Witches of Holy Orchard

Witches of Holy Orchard, Volume 1

Amy Southard

Published by Amy Southard, 2022.

WITCHES OF HOLY ORCHARD

First edition. September 6, 2022.

Copyright © 2022 Amy Southard.

ISBN: 979-8201646561

Written by Amy Southard.

Chapter 1
MERANDA

Sitting in the passenger seat of the blue Hyundai Veloster we rented at the airport, I studied Dad's face. His sand-colored hair and light tanned skin bore no resemblance to mine. Did it ever bother him that Rocco and I both look like mom? *Looked.* He seemed hopeful as I turned the knobs on the radio to find something to drown the silence out; I needed him to not talk to me. A lady was giving the weather forecast and it was the best thing I had heard all day. Suddenly, the sound of the ukulele was like a blow to my diaphragm. *No. Don't look at him.* I momentarily lost my breath and my stomach flopped as if I were falling. Mom's favorite song: the one we played at the funeral.

Somewhere Over the Rainbow, recorded by Israel Kamakawiwoʻoleʻ.

I pretended to not notice the song, but I was paralyzed. I couldn't bring myself to reach up and change the station. I fought it as hard as I could, but I was brought back to that day.

Mom's friend Bane played the song on his ukulele. I watched his fingers strum and pluck the strings as he sang. Tears streamed down his brown face, but his voice never cracked. Bane and Mom were friends since infancy. He was the only person in the world who knew everything about her. Everyone from the island came to see Mom and Rocco laid to rest. All the mourners wore bright colors and their necks adorned with leis.

When it was time to scatter their ashes in the ocean, I couldn't get on my board. Dad, Bane, and some of the other doctors at Mom's hospital got into a yellow canoe and carried their ashes out in gourds. It was a tradition in Mom's family to have a burial at sea. I watched from land, squishing the sand between my toes as Bane's wife Alana hugged my shoulders.

"It's not too late, we can ride out together," she said to me.

"I can't. It should have been me," I said, watching the canoe shrink until it was a yellow blob on the horizon. I collapsed to the ground clenching fists full of wet sand. The scent of salt water enveloped me as my tears mixed with the sea. I stayed there until someone dragged me home when it was over.

I hadn't cried since Mom and Rocco's funeral. I must have cried everything I had until there was nothing left to come out. Suddenly, Dad cleared his throat. The radio was off. How long was I daydreaming? He was talking but I didn't hear what he was saying because I was thinking about home. Dad pulled into an almost empty parking lot next to a brick building with red awnings above the windows.

"Where are we?" I asked.

"Just outside of Boston. This is Vinny's, the pizza place I was telling you about." he said.

"Oh, yeah," I feigned recollection.

Walking in, the aroma of cheese and garlic hugged us at the door. We sat at a table with two chairs and a red gingham tablecloth. I almost thought we were under dressed until I saw the crayons on the table and the man with the goofy mustache on the menu. Dad told the waitress we didn't need the menus. He ordered us both root beers in frosty mugs and a medium pizza with ham and pineapple to share. I prayed that the food would come quickly so I wouldn't have to suffer through conversation.

"You know, they call it a Hawaiian pizza, but it actually originated in Canada. That's why they call the ham Canadian bacon," Dad said to me with his eyebrows raised waiting for a reply.

"Cool," I said in monotone.

About fifteen minutes crawled by slowly as I stared out the window. Dad's words were a baritone melody nearly lulling me to sleep. Finally, our pizza arrived. The scent of warm pineapple flowed from the pizza and commanded me into memory. *We had pineapple on the boat. Rocco loved pineapple. He ate it almost every day, fresh from the trees in our yard. I used to tell him he would turn into a pineapple if he wasn't more careful.* I tried to fight the memory, but it came back to me again.

The sun was orange, and the waves were mellow. Mom was wearing her green and white hibiscus print bathing suit that complimented her long chestnut hair and shimmery tanned skin. Rocco was sitting on the floor of the boat playing with his toy cars and trucks. He was wearing his lime green life vest. Mom was watching him and smiling as the wind blew Rocco's long brown locks into his face.

The clouds rolled in, and the sky darkened suddenly. The waves, now jagged, crashed hard against the side of the boat.

"Meranda, it's about time we head home," Mom said to me.

"Mana, it's time for home," Rocco repeated.

I turned to pull up the anchor just as a wave hit the side of the boat with such force that I was sent flying into the ocean. I landed hard on my back against the water and the wind was knocked out of me. Struggling to resurface and catch my breath, I fought hard to get my head above the water. I desperately tried to make it back to the boat and yelled for Mom, who I thought was probably already throwing the life preserver out to me; she wasn't there. My view inside the boat was blocked, so I was unsure if Rocco was still there.

In a panic I searched the surface of the water but all I could see were waves. I took in a deep breath and went under searching for Mom and Rocco, but I couldn't see them. I came up for air and repeated my search three more times. Nothing. The last time I came up, the lime green of Rocco's life vest bobbed on the horizon. I swam furiously the fifty feet to the vest but as I got closer, Rocco wasn't in it. My baby brother was gone. Mom was gone. There was a sharp pain at the back of my head, and everything went dark.

"Meranda, I think you will really like it in Holy Orchard if you give it a chance. You have an entire family: a grandmother, aunts and cousins who can't wait to meet you," Dad said, snapping me out of my daydream. I continued to stare out the window refusing to acknowledge that I heard my dad speaking to me. *If they are so great, why did it take fifteen years and losing Mom and Rocco for you to tell me about them?* "Honey, you will still be able to surf, it will just be a little different from what you are used to. I loved Massachusetts when I was your age," Dad said trying to convince me I had something to look forward to. *Hence why you left?*

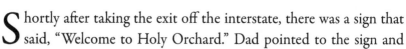

Shortly after taking the exit off the interstate, there was a sign that said, "Welcome to Holy Orchard." Dad pointed to the sign and said, "Meranda! Look! We're almost there!"

I was horrified to see the part that said, "Population 981." *Could this get any worse?*

"Dad?! There's only 981 people in this town?" I grumbled.

"Well, now there's 983," he said using his dad humor.

We slowed to stop at a stop sign and there were rows of big houses with lots of windows. Every yard seemed to have an apple tree or two in it. We took a right on Apple Tree Road. *Really? How original.* We drove up on what must have been the main street in town because we quickly came upon store fronts. They were beautiful old buildings that looked like they had been maintained well. Fresh paint and no cracks like I would expect of something so old. Dad pointed out all the places that this or that happened, but I was not interested in listening.

An elderly man was mowing a lawn, two girls riding their bikes, and a woman in yoga pants walked a golden retriever.

"Up here on the right, the blue one," Dad said pointing to a large blue Victorian house with white trim. He pulled into the driveway and a woman with blond curly hair stepped out onto the porch. "We're here."

Chapter 2
MERANDA

Dad turned off the ignition and popped the trunk with the press of a button. We both got out of the car, and I looked around at my new home. Apparently, the blond woman was my grandma. She didn't look like what I imagined a grandma to look like. She had long curly blond hair with the start of crow's feet in the corners of her eyes. She was wearing a yellow and blue floral summer dress and flip flops. The way she ran to the car and hugged my dad, I knew she couldn't be anyone but my grandma.

"Oh, Nathan! My Nathan is home!" she cried, with a single tear gliding down her cheek. "And Meranda! My beautiful granddaughter! You look just like your mother!" she said hugging me tight. *She knew my mom.* I was usually uncomfortable around strangers, but I was at ease in her arms. I took in a deep breath and inhaled the intoxicating scent of her. Lavender. It was strange like I had known her my whole life.

Grandma held me out in front of her, smiling, "You have such a lovely tan. Are you hungry? I baked banana bread. Do you like apple pie? I have a roast in the crock pot."

I felt strange. I was so angry and hostile moments before arriving, but suddenly I felt... pleasant? Maybe it was the calming effects of the lavender that swirled around me when Grandma hugged me, or maybe everything wasn't as terrible as I thought it was. I took too long pondering my sudden change in emotion and forgot that Grandma had asked me a question.

"Don't be rude. Answer your grandmother," Dad said.

"Oh, Darling. She isn't being rude. She is just taking in her new surroundings. Come inside, sweetheart. I will show you to your room. You are probably exhausted after that flight. How long was it?" Grandma asked as she took my hand to guide me inside.

"Umm, eighteen and a half hours if you count the layover in Seattle," I said as I followed her inside.

"Was it your first time on an airplane?" Grandma asked.

"Yes. I'm not a fan," I grumbled.

Grandma smiled with a look of empathy. "I never enjoyed flying either," she said as she stopped in the entry way. "This is the foyer. We hang our coats in here on these hooks. It's nice and warm out now, but it gets cold in the winter. We take our shoes off in here, too."

Grandma slid off her flip flops, while Dad and I followed her lead. I set my sandals next to hers and Dad set his next to mine. Grandma took my hand again and led me into the room to the left.

"This is the living room," Grandma said, pausing to allow me to look around.

The floor was beautiful hardwood. It was dark colored, but I wasn't sure what kind. Black walnut maybe, but I was no expert. There was a blue sofa and two chairs to match. White curtains with large blue flowers framed the sides of a giant window overlooking the front yard. An empty fireplace sat at the end of the room and a painting of four children hung above it. Grandma noticed me staring at the painting.

"Ah, I had that painting done of the only photograph that existed with all four of my children in it. My sweet Sarah passed away in infancy," Grandma said with a glossiness in her eyes and a slight crack in her voice. My intuition told me she was remembering something sad.

"Sarah? Dad is that where I got my middle name?" I asked, suddenly intrigued.

"Yes, your mother and I agreed to name you Meranda Sarah after my mother and baby sister who was only with us a short time," Dad said.

"Your name is Meranda, too?" I asked, turning to face my grandma.

"It sure is, my dear. I was enormously proud when your dad told me he was naming you after me," she said, smiling.

There was an opening, and I took it. "Why didn't my dad tell me about you?" I asked, as if he wasn't standing right there. "Why weren't you in my life?"

Dad opened his mouth as his face transformed into surprise and anger. I was sure he was going to yell or scold me, but Grandma put her hand up to stop him before he could speak.

"Darling, your dad and I weren't on the best of terms when you were born. Please don't be angry with him. There will be plenty of time to talk about the past, but it's all water under the bridge. I am just so excited to have the two of you home and I am looking forward to introducing you to the rest of your family. They want to let you get settled in first, though. They are coming for dinner tomorrow."

I wanted to ask more questions. I wanted to hear more, but Grandma's words were enough. At least for that moment. After a brief pause, Grandma smiled and continued the tour. She led us through to the library which doubled as her office. It smelled inviting, like old books and patchouli. There was a reading nook with large pink cushions. I noticed a lamp with a gold base and a white and floral shade. We didn't spend much time in there, but I would check it out later when I had more time to myself.

Grandma seemed to sense the moment I became too tired to enjoy the tour. "How about I show you to your room, so you can take a nap before dinner? I can show you the rest of the house later," she said sweetly.

I yawned and nodded as she led me up a staircase lined with a wall of family photos. I held onto the banister and followed closely up the stairs. My dad followed behind us.

"Nathan, your room is where you left it. You are free to redecorate if you choose. I kept everything the same," Grandma said with a little sadness in her voice as Dad walked ahead and went to his room. She seemed to snap out of it quickly and smiled as she looked back at me. "Your aunt Sarah's old room sat empty for many years after she died. We used it as a nursery for your cousins when they lived here. It's been several years since it's been used. Maybe you can liven it up again. When you are feeling up to it, we can go shopping for some things to make it more personal."

Grandma led me down a hall of rooms. We passed a large painting of red and orange flowers. "Those are poppies. My favorite flower. Your grandfather Samuel painted it for me, many years ago," she said smiling like she was remembering fondly.

"Where is he?" I asked. "My grandfather?"

"Oh, my dear, he passed away when your dad was a little boy. He had a bad heart. He was a good man and an amazing painter. You would have loved him," she said.

At the end of the hall was an open door. Grandma led me through it. "Like I said, we can go shopping later this week and redecorate. You just get settled in and I will be downstairs in the kitchen. The bathroom is right across the hall and your dad's room is next to that." Grandma smiled and closed the door gently.

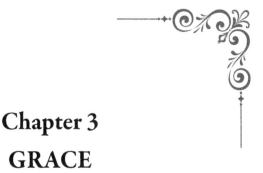

Chapter 3
GRACE

S taring up at the ceiling, I laid down on my freshly made four-poster bed, holding Tinkerbell on my chest. Tinkerbell was a fuzzy orange kitten that I had been fostering. She lost her mother and needed to be bottle fed around the clock. Her eyes weren't even open yet when I got her, but at that moment they were as blue as sapphire. As I looked deeply into Tink's eyes, the sapphire around the psychic's neck came into memory.

Emily, Bess, Olivia, and I walked through the gate of the County Fair. The fragrant smell of barnyard and fried food was in the air. We were on a mission as we walked past the Ferris wheel and straight on to the psychic's trailer. The sounds of laughter and delighted fearful screams surrounded us as the sun disappeared below the horizon. Genevieve the Psychic was dressed like a cheesy fortune teller. The door of her trailer had a purple and blue beaded curtain, and she was robed like a gypsy in gold and blue. A large sapphire pendant dangled from her neck.

Olivia, known to us as "Liv," had no confidence in Genevieve the Psychic. She complained the whole way to the fair and was agitated the entire time. The rest of us were confident in Genevieve's abilities. We did our research. Genevieve was an expert, and she was difficult to find, but we found her.

She invited us into her trailer. A pullout bed was open in the back with several boxes stacked on top. The table had a square of green velour draped over it like a tablecloth and there was a fancy crystal ball in the middle. Genevieve excused herself to use the restroom and asked us to wait. Liv suggested we not waste our money and ditch while the psychic was gone.

"This is stupid. We are really going to pay this lady thirty dollars apiece to give us some generic reading that she gives everyone who comes to see her?" *Liv whispered.*

Bess started to lose her nerve as well. "Maybe she's right. She looks like a phony."

"I promise, if this doesn't work, I will personally reimburse all of your money. This is going to work; I can feel it. She is going to know something." *I pleaded with the group.*

Tinkerbell purred loudly as she curled up to my neck. I gently cradled her and brought her over to the pet carrier I had been keeping her in. I laid her on the blue fleece blanket and closed the carrier door. A wooden box with a triquetra carved into the top sat on top of my vanity. I walked over, opened the lid, and peered inside. My money was stashed in that box and at that moment I had $300 in tips I saved from my summer job waitressing at the café. It was time I accepted the fact that I had to reimburse my friends the cost of that psychic. I plopped down on my bed defeated, remembering what the psychic said.

"Your magic is not powerful enough because you are missing a person. There is another witch who is destined to be part of your coven. With her, your magic will be much stronger," *Genevieve the psychic said.*

"Really? How do we find her?" *I asked as I leaned closer.*

"Well, you wait. As I said, she is destined to come, she is just far away and completely unaware that she is a witch," *Genevieve replied as she pushed her chair back to stand.*

"How do you know this?" *Liv asked in a snotty tone, glaring at the psychic.*

"You don't have to believe me, but I am a psychic and you girls came to me, remember?"

"There is really nothing we can do to find her?" Emily asked sincerely.

"Well, I suppose you could do a spell to call a lost witch, but we are out of time. I have a line waiting."

Everyone stood up as Genevieve walked to the door of the trailer to lead us out.

"Do you have a spell to call a lost witch?" I asked before she opened the door.

"What kind of witches are you? Do you not have a Book of Shadows or mothers or grandmothers who have practiced magic? Surely you can figure out how to call a witch?" She said rushing us out the door.

My cell phone chimed to alert me of an incoming text. I recognized the tone as the one I had set for Liv and expected it to be a text demanding the money I owed her for the psychic. We found a spell to call a lost witch in the Grimoire my grandmother gave me before she died last year. We performed the ritual and spell in the woods the day after we visited the psychic at the fair.

There was a note in Grandmother's handwriting that said if the spell worked, our missing witch would come to us within two weeks. That night would be two weeks exactly and there had been no sign of our missing witch. I looked at my phone to read Liv's text and found that she was only asking me to cover her shift at the café tomorrow morning. I replied, "Yes."

Car doors slammed outside. It sounded like someone was at my house. Mrs. Wickstrom from next door shouted excitedly, "Oh, Nathan! My Nathan is home! And Meranda! My beautiful granddaughter! You look just like your mother!"

I ran to my window and looked to my neighbor's house. There was a man and a teenage girl about my age standing in the driveway next door. She had long brown hair and tan skin. She was wearing a blue t-shirt with writing that I couldn't read and khaki shorts. *It worked. That has to be her!*

Chapter 4
MERANDA

The walls were papered in a sage green with pink roses. I didn't mind it. I looked around the room and every piece of furniture was white. There was a full size four poster bed with pink and green bedding. It was so inviting after my long flight and car ride. I sat down on the bed and noticed the mirror on the vanity across the room. My reflection was tired, staring back at me. *I do look like my mom.*

Exhaustion was creeping in, but I wanted to explore everything. I got up and searched around in all the drawers of the dresser and the vanity. I opened the wardrobe cabinet. That was empty too. I walked over to the window on the other side of the bed and found several packages addressed to my grandma from Hawaii. I almost forgot we sent some of my things. I opened the first box and smiled as Rocco's stuffed cheetah stood out among my journal, a stack of neatly folded t-shirts, a framed photo of me and my best friend Leilani, and the boho bag she made for me as a going away present. My tears streamed quickly down my face, but I continued smiling.

After rummaging through my things for about twenty minutes, I needed to take that nap. I pulled back the duvet and pushed some of the overstuffed pillows off to the side. I laid down, hugged Rocco's cheetah to my chest, and closed my eyes. When I opened them, my grandma was standing over the bed smiling.

"Grandma! You startled me!" I said, my voice shaking.

"Oh dear, I am sorry. I didn't want to let you sleep too much longer. You already missed dinner and you slept all through the night," Grandma said as I sat up.

"It's morning?" I asked, almost not believing her.

"You slept so soundly. I unpacked your suitcases and put your clothes in the wardrobe. I hope you don't mind. I wanted it to feel like you've moved in."

"No, I don't mind. I can't believe I didn't wake up. I am usually such a light sleeper," I said, still amazed that it was morning.

"I knew you were tired. It was almost magical how deeply you were sleeping. Anyway, your dad wants to take us to breakfast at Ruth's Café downtown. They have home cooking almost as good as mine. Hop in the shower and come down when you are ready. Take your time, dear."

Grandma left my room and closed the door behind her. I set Rocco's cheetah on the vanity and searched in the filled wardrobe for something to wear. A red summer dress with large white flowers on it stood out from the rest. *Works for me.* I selected a clean white bra and panties, then I headed for the door.

The bathroom was across the hall from my room. I walked in and instantly noticed the teal brick-style tiles and the white claw-footed tub in the middle of the room near the window. There was a white sink on a pedestal, a large mirror above it and a stand-up shower with a glass door in the corner. I closed the bathroom door and got ready for the day.

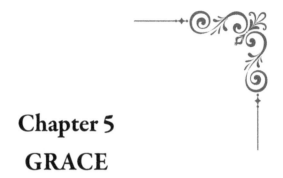

Chapter 5
GRACE

My shift at Ruth's Café started at 5:30 AM. All morning I had the regular customers coming in for coffee and breakfast. Even though I never drank it, I've always loved the smell of coffee and it was extra strong today. Tony rang the bell that signaled one of my orders was ready. I walked up to the window and pulled down two plates of blueberry smile pancakes (two blueberries for the eyes and a slice of bacon for the mouth) and a plate with a veggie omelet with extra cheese for table four.

At table four sat my favorite customers- Mr. Bardley and his six-year-old twins (one boy and one girl.) Bardley and the twins had been coming to Ruth's Café every Sunday morning since they were born, while Mrs. Bardley hosted the weekly Women of Holy Orchard tea at their house. I'd become a pro at carrying three plates at once by resting one of the pancake orders on my arm and balancing carefully all the way to their table. I set Mr. Bardley's plate down first, so that I could use my free hand to grab the plate resting on my arm. I set one order of pancakes in front of Morgan (the girl twin) first and the other plate in front of Brayden (the boy twin.)

"Why do you always give my sister her pancakes first?" Brayden asked me.

"Well, because she's always sitting the farthest away. It wouldn't be polite to reach over your food to give her a plate, would it?" I asked.

Brayden stared at me quizzically and announced to the table that he would be sitting by the wall next week. Everyone laughed then happily took their first bites of food.

"Let me know if you need a refill on your orange juice," I said as I walked away. I almost forgot about our missing witch, Meranda, but she kept popping back into my mind. I texted Bess, Emily, and Liv last night to tell them. They all agreed that we needed to meet her before we would believe it was really her.

The bells on the door chimed to alert me that a customer had come in. Meranda was standing there with her father and Mrs. Wickstrom. They quickly selected a booth and sat down. Butterflies fluttered in my stomach as I grabbed three menus and rushed over to their table.

Chapter 6
MERANDA

After I finished my shower and was ready for the day, it was nearly nine AM. Dad said he wanted to treat me and Grandma to breakfast at Ruth's Café. It was funny that the whole reason we had to move was because we didn't have any money but, somehow, he could treat us to breakfast. I didn't comment on that.

Dad wanted us to walk to the café because it was only a few blocks away. The houses were nothing like the ones back home in Hawaii. They were all two or three stories, some with bay windows, many with gables or towers. There was a house painted black. I had never in my life seen a black house before. The lady was out walking the golden retriever again. Grandma waved and yelled a greeting.

After we walked a couple of blocks, I commented that there were a lot of apple trees. Grandma and Dad opened their mouths to talk at the same time, but Dad stayed silent and allowed Grandma to go first.

"Well, they call the town Holy Orchard for a reason. Most of what makes up Holy Orchard today was actually an apple orchard owned by the first mayor of the town back in the 1600's. Eli Wickstrom," Grandma said.

"Wickstrom? One of our ancestors?" I asked, genuinely interested.

"Nathan, you never told her our history?" Grandma asked with her eyebrows lowered.

Dad shrugged, and Grandma continued.

"Yes, our ancestor. Eli Wickstrom was very wealthy. He came from England and was one of the town's founders. He and his brother Giles, along with a good friend Henry Archer, came to Massachusetts and brought with them sacks of apple seeds," Grandma said proudly.

"Cool. So, they started an orchard?" I asked.

"They purchased a large piece of land which is what we recognize today as Holy Orchard. They planted thousands of apple seeds. They called the town Holy Orchard because the first building to be constructed was a church. I'll show it to you. Just around the corner. You can see the bell tower just over those trees," Grandma said excitedly as she pointed.

"It's still standing?" I asked, amazed.

"It's been restored and is a museum now. People rent it out for weddings. Your aunt Lily got married there years ago. Oh! There it is! The bell still rings every day at noon," Grandma said, pointing at an old but nicely maintained brick church with white doors.

"And there is Ruth's Café," Dad said, pointing to the café at the end of the block. Next to the church was a veterinarian's office, then a thrift store. I made a mental note to check out the thrift store one of these days when I have money. Next to the thrift store was a bicycle repair shop, followed by Ruth's Café. Across the street was Holy Orchard Public Library, which took up the whole block. *Another place to check out later.*

Ruth's Café was a small brick building with green and white awnings. There was a large patio to the side with tables, chairs, and umbrellas. A sign stuck out from above the door that said "Ruth's Café" in cursive neon lights over top an outline of a coffee cup with steam coming out of it. I took in a deep breath and the smell of fresh coffee, bacon and eggs went straight to my stomach. My mouth watered and a deep growl came from my abdomen.

Dad opened the door and Grandma and I walked in. There were bells on the door that chimed when we walked in and a teenage waitress with wavy blond hair looked up and hurried to get menus for us.

"Oh, that's the girl from next door. Grace. She is lovely! I will introduce you!" Grandma said, tapping my arm excitedly as Dad led us to a booth.

We had barely sat down, and Grace was already at the table with our menus.

"Hello Mrs. Wickstrom! Would you like to hear the breakfast specials before I take your drink orders?" Grace asked.

"Oh, no. Thank you, dear. Grace, I'd like you to meet my son Nathan and my granddaughter Meranda. They will be living with me for a while," Grandma said.

Grace put her notepad and pen in the front pocket of her apron and reached out to shake our hands.

"Oh, it's so nice to meet you! Where did you move here from?" she asked politely.

"We moved here from Hawaii," I said as nicely as I could.

"Why would anyone move to the East coast from Hawaii?" Grace asked, shocked.

The question caught me off guard and I blurted out that my mom and brother died two weeks earlier. Grandma raised her brows and Dad elbowed me in the side. Why did I blurt that out? *Idiot.* I was in a new place and didn't know anyone. My whole world just got flipped upside down and it was the first thing that popped into my head.

"Oh, my goodness! I am so sorry for your loss!" Grace said sympathetically. I thanked her, and we sat in a brief awkward silence looking from one another to Grace, until finally my dad spoke up.

"Actually, I think we would like to hear the breakfast specials."

"Alright," Grace said, taking the pen and notepad from her apron. As Grace went over the specials, I silently scolded myself for telling a stranger the absolute worst thing that's ever happened to me, within the first few minutes of meeting her.

"Would you like to try one of those?" Grace asked politely.

"Thank you, Grace. I think we might need a few minutes, but I will take a coffee in the meantime," Dad said.

"I will have a caramel iced coffee, please, and a water," I said.

"Great, and could I get you a spearmint lemon grass tea, Mrs. Wickstrom?" she asked. Grandma nodded and smiled as Grace was already starting to walk away.

Grace quickly returned with our drinks and asked if we were ready to order. I already knew what I wanted, so I looked to Grandma and Dad.

"Dear, before we order, I just wanted to tell you that Meranda will be enrolled at the high school, and she doesn't know anyone yet. Since school doesn't start for another week, I was hoping you could show her around and introduce her to some of your friends. She is going into tenth grade, too," Grandma said as heat rushed to my cheeks. I was humiliated.

"Oh, yes! Yes, I would love to," Grace said, and I wasn't sure if she was genuinely excited for the opportunity to show the new kid around or if she was just being polite. "My shift ends at noon. Will you be home around one?" She asked.

I looked to Dad and Grandma because I wasn't sure what they had planned for me. I was nervous, but I was also getting tired of Dad acting like everything was just peachy keen. If I could get out of talking to him for a few more hours, I'd feel a little bit better.

"Oh, that would be lovely. She will be home by one, so you just stop by when you are ready," Grandma said, pleased.

Grandma and I ordered the avocado toast special on marble rye bread and Dad had a vegetarian omelet with hash browns. Breakfast went extremely fast. We didn't do much talking once our food arrived. Poor Grandma was used to eating hours earlier but waited for us. I hadn't eaten since we stopped at that pizza place the day before. I'm guessing Dad hadn't eaten since dinner, but I didn't really care. My mind was swirling with questions like, "Does Grace really want to show me around?" and "What are Grace and her friends like?" Maybe Holy Orchard wouldn't be so bad after all.

Chapter 7
GRACE

It had to be her. I could just feel it. Meranda had to be the lost witch we called. I couldn't stop thinking about her and what brought her to Holy Orchard. She said that her mother and brother died two weeks ago, so they had to move here from Hawaii. That cannot be a coincidence. We did our spell to call a lost witch two weeks ago. Did we unintentionally make her family die? Genevieve the Psychic told us to wait, and she would eventually find her way to us, but we had to be impatient and do a spell to make her come sooner. What if we did this?

The second Jane came in for her shift, I clocked out and pulled my phone from my purse. I texted Emily, Bess, and Liv. I'm not usually one to walk and text, but this was important. I nearly got hit by a car when I was crossing Apple Tree Road.

Group text with you, Emily, Bess, and Liv

Me: OMG! She came in 2 Ruth's while I was working! I'm meeting her at 1 to show her around n introduce her 2 ppl.

Liv: It's probably not even her. Don't get ur hopes up.

Emily: OMG! It's her! I know it! I can just feel it guys!

Bess: Really? What will u say to her?

Me: IDK. I mean I can't just ask if she is a witch.

Emily: The psychic said she doesn't know.

Emily: She probably doesn't know she is one.

Emily: It's her I bet. I can feel it.

Me: She said her mother and brother died 2 weeks ago.

Me: I think we caused it.

Bess: OMG!

Bess: What if we caused it?

Bess: How did they die?

Emily: Yeah, how did they die?

Me: IDK. I got to find out.

Me: OMG! I almost got hit by a car.

Me: I need 2 stop texting.

Me: I'll tell you everything, but I need 2 get there. TTYL.

Liv: ttyl

Bess: TTYL

Emily: Keep us posted. TTYL.

I couldn't wait any longer. The suspense was killing me. I had to find out everything about Meranda Wickstrom. I ran the rest of the way home, showered the smell of food away and rushed next door. I walked up the steps and rang the doorbell at 12:42.

Chapter 8

MERANDA

After we finished at the café, we took the same route home. I asked Grandma if my aunt Lily had any children and when I would meet them.

"She has three boys. Aidan and Zayden are twins, and they are eight. Jaxon is six," Grandma said.

"The whole family is planning to come over tomorrow night for dinner," Dad said. I thought I was doing a good job of masking my annoyance, but realized when Dad looked down at his feet, that I was glaring at him.

"I asked them to give you a couple of days to get used to everything," Grandma said reassuringly.

I remembered Dad and Grandma saying I had aunts, plural. "What about my other aunt?" I asked.

"Yes, your aunt Rachel. You will meet her tomorrow, too. She has two sons. Dean is sixteen and Max is thirteen. Dean is going into tenth grade, too. So, you will at least have a couple of friends when you start school between Dean and Grace," Grandma said like she was trying to convince me.

I barely paid attention to anything as we walked home. It was strange to call this place home. Hawaii was the only home I ever had. Grandma said I would at least have two friends between Grace and Dean, but I didn't know either one of them. Leilani was my friend. I was homesick again.

Dad excused himself to go out job searching and left me alone with Grandma. That was fine with me because I couldn't stand to see his face anymore that day. Dad should have been there on the boat. He was supposed to be there. I couldn't save Mom and Rocco because I was knocked out, but he could have. He should have. Everyone kept telling me I couldn't blame myself. Well fine. I would just blame him instead.

I sat down at the kitchen table as angry tears streamed down my face. Grandma rushed in almost immediately like she knew what I was doing in there.

"Oh dear, you can't hold things in. Let's talk about it. I'll make us some tea," Grandma said, grabbing an English rose tea kettle from the cabinet and filling it with water.

"No thanks, Grandma. I am not really a fan of tea," I said reaching for a tissue from the box that mysteriously showed up on the table after Grandma came in.

"I promise, you will like it. It will make you feel better. Please? Just try it," Grandma said, her eyebrows raised waiting for me to give in.

"Okay, I will try a cup," I acquiesced, then wiped my nose.

After Grandma poured two cups of tea and added honey to mine, she sat across from me at the table. I took a sip of tea, and it didn't taste too bad. It warmed my chest instantly and I was a little calmer. Grandma reached across the table and put her hand on mine.

"Your heart is broken. It will hurt for a long while, but in time it will hurt less and less," Grandma said in a soothing tone. "You will think of them and smile instead of cry. You will let go of your anger," she said with confidence. "I lost my husband and while I was still grieving for him, I lost my sweet Sarah. I had to raise three children on my own and they were sad, too," Grandma said as she looked into my eyes. It was like she was peering into my soul.

"How did you get through it?" I asked, no longer crying.

"One day at a time. I also took comfort in knowing that their bodies were feeding the Earth. I immersed myself in gardening. I also started journaling and writing poetry. I cooked everything from scratch. My kids had the healthiest meals in town," Grandma paused like she was deep in thought. "You need to forgive him. It will only hurt you to hold on to that anger."

Her comment surprised me. How did she know I was angry at my dad? I guessed maybe he told her, or maybe she could just sense it. I thought I was suppressing it well, but maybe I wasn't.

"He should have been there. He was supposed to be there, but he ditched us to go golfing with some guy he was trying to impress at work. If he had been there..." I trailed off, trying to stop the tears from forming again.

"Don't you think he's beating himself up over that? He couldn't have possibly known something like that was going to happen or he would have been there. Your dad would have done anything to protect his family. You have to understand that," Grandma said softly. "Now drink up before your tea gets cold."

I finished my tea and my mood improved. Suddenly, loud church bells rang in the distance. Grandma and I looked up at each other and smiled.

"It's noon. I've heard those church bells every day at noon since the day I was born. Every time I hear them, I get the urge to go out in the yard and admire my garden. Come with me?" Grandma said taking my hand. I followed her through the sliding glass doors out onto the back patio. There were pots of flowers everywhere. Large pots. Small pots. Hanging pots.

Down the stairs there was a path that curled around a small vegetable garden and every kind of flower I could imagine. There were sunflowers, snapdragons, poppies, rose bushes, a trellis with white and blue flowers climbing up. Along the garden shed was a row of hollyhocks. I watched as a bee landed on Grandma's hand. She looked at the bee in silence for several moments.

"It's okay. He just needs a little rest, and he knows my hand is a safe place to stop. He will fly off in a minute. It's the least I could do for someone who pollinates my garden for me," Grandma said.

I never heard a bee referred to as "someone" before. My grandma was an interesting person. I had just met her, but I already loved her.

After spending some time in the garden, we went back inside. Moments later the doorbell rang.

"Ah. 12:42," Grandma said, looking at her watch, "that would be Grace. That girl has never been late a day in her life. You can always count on her to be early."

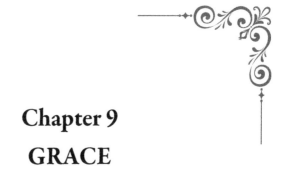

Chapter 9
GRACE

Mrs. Wickstrom opened the door with a smile after only a few seconds.

"Grace, hello! Come in, dear," Mrs. Wickstrom said ushering me in. I thanked her and stepped inside, sliding my shoes off in the foyer. She led me to the kitchen and gestured for me to sit at the table. I had spent many afternoons drinking tea in her kitchen when my grandmother was still alive. I learned a lot about gardening from them.

"So, what are we going to do?" Meranda asked me.

"Well, I was thinking..." just then I remembered Tinkerbell. "Oh, my goodness! I forgot to feed Tinkerbell when I got home! She's too young to be away from her mother, so I have to bottle feed her," I said as I made my way back to the door. "Meranda, is it OK if we go to my house and hang out while I feed my foster kitten?" I asked. I was angry at myself. I never forgot to care for my fosters before.

"Yeah. That sounds good," Meranda said, following me to the foyer. Mrs. Wickstrom told us to have fun, we got our shoes on and went out the door.

Chapter 10
MERANDA

Grace seemed really flustered and it was obvious she was upset about forgetting to feed her cat. I didn't understand why it was such a big deal, but apparently Grace took her fostering very seriously. I followed her next door. Grace's home was a modest two-story brick house that was painted white with black accents. Of course, there was an apple tree in the front yard.

Grace's room was on the second floor at the front of the house, with a window facing the street. When we walked in, Grace went straight to a pet carrier on the floor in her very purple room. Frantic mews came from the orange ball of fur that Grace pulled out of the carrier.

"I'm so sorry, I forgot to feed you, baby girl. I will never do that again, I promise!" She said as she held the kitten to her chest, petting it. Grace told me to have a seat and gestured to her bed. Everything was purple in her room. Her walls were painted a shade of lavender and her bedspread was white with lilacs all over it. She had several throw pillows in different shades of purple and a large purple faux fur rug. I sat down on her bed and examined the titles on her bookshelf.

Grace sat down next to me with a bottle of kitten milk replacer and fed Tinkerbell. "Do you like to read?" she asked, noticing that I was looking at her books.

"Sometimes. You have a lot of gardening and animal care books," I said.

"I actually learned to garden from your grandmother. Well, and mine too. They were best friends, but my grandmother passed away last year. And I love animals. I always find the ones that need help the most and take them in," Grace said as she gazed lovingly at Tinkerbell.

"Cool," I said, not sure what to say next.

"Tinkerbell usually falls asleep after I feed her, so we can go somewhere else. Or we can just sit here and talk. Whatever you want."

"We could just talk if you want. Do you play soccer?" I asked, peering at the shelf of trophies and medals across the room.

"I used to. I haven't played since my father died," she said. I could sense her heart beating faster and a lump developed in my throat.

"When did he die?" I asked. I already shared with her that my mom and brother died two weeks ago, so I didn't think I was prying.

"It was two years ago in a plane crash. He traveled a lot for business. He was on his way home from Alaska and his plane crashed right after taking off. So, when you said your mother and brother passed away, I understand how you feel."

"I'm sorry to hear about that. My mom and brother Rocco drowned," I said, unsure how much I should share.

"In the ocean?"

"Well, we were spending the day on the boat having a picnic and a bad storm suddenly came in out of nowhere," I said, the hot tears forming behind my eyes. "I got knocked into the water and almost drowned. When I came up, I couldn't find them." I looked up at Grace, willing myself not to cry. "I assumed they got knocked in, too. I don't really understand what happened. I was knocked unconscious."

Grace looked like *she* was going to cry, "Oh, how awful," she said sincerely.

"Something hit me in the back of the head and knocked me out. I woke up in the hospital and my dad told me they drowned. The storm didn't last very long. We weren't out that far either," I said, considering the strangeness of the events that I had been pondering for two weeks.

"How did you get out of the water if you were unconscious?" Grace asked, stuttering slightly.

"Someone found me washed up on shore and they went searching for Mom and Rocco. They found them later and they had drowned," I said wiping the wetness from my eyes. I glanced up at Grace just in time to see a tear stream down her face. She didn't talk and seemed to be holding her breath, but finally she let out a sigh.

"I'm so sorry. I feel *so* terrible for you and what you went through," Grace said as she got up and put Tinkerbell in the pet carrier.

"Thanks. So, to change the subject to something less sad, what do you and your friends do for fun?" I asked.

Grace sat back down on the bed next to me and said, "Well, we do all kinds of things. Like I said, I love gardening and fostering animals. I have three best friends. Emily, Bess, and Liv. Of course, there's always room for one more." It seemed so natural to be listening to Grace talk about herself and her friends. There was something familiar and comforting about her. She continued, "as you know, I work at the café. Liv's grandmother is Ruth. She owns the café. So, Liv works there, too. Liv is on the swim team. Emily is head cheerleader. Her father is the school principal, and her mother teaches history. We usually go to all the football games to cheer them on. Actually, Dean is on the football team."

"Dean?" I asked, confused.

"Your cousin?" she said.

"Oh, duh. Well, I haven't met him yet, so..."

"I didn't realize. He is pretty cool. Emily has a crush on him. Oh! I shouldn't have said that. Don't tell him," Grace said quickly.

"It's cool. I won't say anything. So, what else? Tell me more," I relaxed a little. Maybe Grace and I would become good friends.

"My other friend Bess is a figure skater. Her father is the chief of police, and her mother is an English teacher at the high school. It's a small town, so you will discover that everyone is connected in some way. We like to go to the movies and to concerts."

"Do Liv's parents work at the school, too?" I asked, since I recognized a pattern forming.

Grace laughed awkwardly, "No, actually, she lives with her grandmother. Her mother is in rehab, and she never knew her father. Maybe don't tell her I told you. It's really her business to tell."

"Ah, right. I won't tell. What about your mom?" I asked.

"She owns Holy Orchard Soaps and Candles. She makes all of the soaps, candles, perfumes and such herself."

"Oh, that's cool," I said.

"Enough about us, what about you? What do you do? Do you play any sports or have any special interests or talents?" she asked sounding extremely interested.

"I love to surf. I was on the swim team. I like sailing. Dancing, going to movies, listening to music. I like all kinds of things," I said. It was awkward talking about myself.

"Oh, you will fit right in. Liv is hoping to make swim team captain this year. I'm sure she wouldn't mind a little bit of friendly competition. So, what about your family? What was it like in Hawaii?" she asked.

"My mom was a pediatric surgeon. Dad wasn't home much. He works in marketing and was always golfing to lure in new clients. Rocco was only two, but I was really close to him. I babysat him a lot. My best friend Leilani and I were teaching him to swim," I said, hating myself momentarily. I'd failed him.

Grace's phone chimed a notification that she had a text message. She looked at her phone and with a smile said, "My friends want to meet you."

Chapter 11
GRACE

Meranda told me the specific details about the death of her mother and brother. I felt extremely responsible and couldn't hold back the single tear that escaped. Seeing her cry made me emotional. Partly because I had immense guilt over the death of her family and partly because I am an empath. I had gotten particularly good at controlling my emotions around other people, so that I am not a basket case everywhere I go, but today was hard. I was sensing such deep sadness and despair from her. I could feel the loss like it was my own. The emptiness. The heavy ball at the bottom of my sternum. The same as when my father died two years ago and my grandmother, just last year.

I was relieved when Meranda suggested a change to more pleasant conversation. I wanted to make myself and my friends sound as appealing as I could, without sounding conceited. I wanted her to like us. I wanted her to join our coven. By the time my phone chimed with a message from Bess saying the girls wanted to meet her, I was already sure that Meranda was our lost witch.

When Meranda explained the details of the boating accident, the timing was too perfect. A storm came in suddenly and left just as quick. As if it were caused by outside forces and not Mother Nature herself. Meranda was knocked from the boat and nearly drowned. She even lost consciousness when something hit her in the back of the head.

Surely, she would have drowned. Only something like magic could have saved her. Maybe she was able to manipulate and control the water element, like Liv can. They both enjoy water sports. Maybe Meranda saved herself from drowning by controlling the ocean while she was unconscious. I would have to tell my friends about my theory later.

I told Meranda that my friends wanted to meet her, and I instantly felt her emotions change. I sensed nervousness and fear from her.

"Right now?" she asked with alarm in her voice.

"Oh, not if you don't want to. We can wait for another day. I'll text them not to come," I said, hoping I hadn't scared her off.

"No, that's fine. I just need to rip the bandage off," she said, relaxing into my throw pillows and taking a deep breath.

"Yeah, it will be fine. They are great girls. I wouldn't be friends with them if they weren't. I think we will all get along great," I said, believing it was true.

"I don't have a lot of female friends. I usually make friends more easily with guys," she said as she hugged one of my pillows to her chest.

It didn't take long for them to arrive. Meranda and I were deep in conversation about our favorite television shows (neither of us watch much television apparently) when we were startled by the sound of three bikes falling to the ground outside my window. Bess, Emily, and Liv didn't bother knocking and came straight upstairs to my room.

Bess was the first to enter, wearing denim shorts and a black and maroon floral tank top, with her long brown hair up in a messy bun. "Hi, I'm Bess," she said, smiling widely. Sensing her emotions as she walked in the door made me incredibly happy. I was thankful for Bess because she was so pleasant to be around.

Behind her came Emily, wearing black yoga capri pants and a blue "Holy Orchard Football Cheerleaders" t-shirt. Her long red hair was worn down and tucked behind her ears. She didn't immediately introduce herself, so I took the honor of doing so. Meranda smiled and nodded her head.

Liv came into the room, and I sensed some hostility from her. She had a smile on her face as if she were happy, but my empath power told me otherwise. Liv had a dark brown pixie cut and had each ear pierced half a dozen times. She wore tight faded jeans with holes in the knees and a "Holy Orchard High Swim" t-shirt.

"And lastly, this is Liv. She is the one on the swim team," I said.

Meranda set the pillow down and stood up, "It's nice to meet you all."

Chapter 12
MERANDA

My first week in Holy Orchard went okay. I had spent every day with Grace since we met. Her friends Bess and Emily were nice. Liv didn't talk much and always had other plans. It was difficult leaving Grandma when I could have been getting to know her better, but she insisted I needed to make friends.

The evening I first met Grace, I came home to find my aunts and cousins visiting. Grandma had prepared a feast in the formal dining room, and it wasn't as awkward as I thought it would be. I had expected all eyes to be on me, but after the initial greeting and some occasional questions from everyone, the conversation was equally spread. My aunt Rachel looked a lot like Dad and Grandma, with blond hair and light skin. Aunt Lily had red hair and freckles. She must have gotten her looks from my grandfather. I made a mental note to ask Grandma to see pictures of him later.

My younger cousins: Jaxon, Zayden and Aidan (I still couldn't remember who was who) were pretty rambunctious and deserted the table to wrestle in the living room. Dean and Max were older and more civilized. Grandma asked Dean about football and Dad said he was excited to go to all his games. Dean and my dad got along well. I found out by listening to Aunt Rachel and Dad talking that Dean and Max lost their father almost ten years ago. Then, Aunt Lily said that her husband died six years ago, and Jaxon hadn't even gotten to meet his father.

One thing I had in common with all my cousins, was the loss of a parent. Even Grace had lost her father. I was sad for them. I wouldn't wish the loss of a parent on anyone. It was a little nice, though, to believe that I will probably survive.

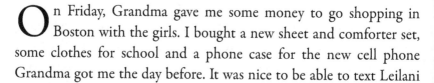

On Friday, Grandma gave me some money to go shopping in Boston with the girls. I bought a new sheet and comforter set, some clothes for school and a phone case for the new cell phone Grandma got me the day before. It was nice to be able to text Leilani again.

Monday was an open house at Holy Orchard High. Students were able to get their class schedules and locker numbers, and new students were able to get a tour of the school. I went with Grace and the girls. School was starting the next day and I didn't want to get lost on my first day.

After getting our schedules, we sat down at a table in the commons. The school was a lot bigger than my old school. In Hawaii, I went to a small charter school. We were lucky we had a swim team. In comparison, this place was huge.

"Why do you seem so surprised?" Bess asked, as she sat next to me at the table.

"This school is way bigger than I thought it would be. I believed small town meant small school," I said.

"This school district services students in at least five other towns. It is closer for students to commute to Holy Orchard, rather than go all the way to Boston," Grace said, matter-of-factually.

"You have my mom for English!" Bess said, pointing at my schedule.

"What hour? I have her second hour," Grace said, eagerly waiting for my reply.

"Oh, second hour for me, too," I said.

We spent the next several minutes comparing schedules. It turned out that Grace and I had almost every class together. The only class I had with Emily was P.E. last hour. Everyone except Liv was in PE with us. The one class I didn't have with Grace was fifth hour.

"Liv, what do you have fifth hour? Meranda has World History with Chisholm, but Bess and I have World History with Emily's mom and Emily has Spanish two," Grace asked facing Liv.

"Ah, guess I have Chisholm that hour, too. Awesome," Liv said. I couldn't tell if she was being sarcastic or not, but I was relieved. *Thank Goodness.* I'd have someone I knew in every class.

We spent the next hour or so walking around the school, finding our classes and our lockers. The tenth-grade lockers were all down the same hall and organized alphabetically. That meant that my cousin Dean's locker would be right next to mine, and Grace was only a few away from me in the next group of lockers because her last name is Ziegler.

———— ❧ ————

Later that night, I sat at the table drinking tea with Grandma. We talked about how nervous I was for school the next day and she suggested, or rather insisted I take a bath.

"I don't really like taking baths. I'd feel like I'm sitting in dirt soup," I said, drinking down the last of the chamomile and honey tea Grandma had made for me.

"Oh, I promise you will enjoy it. Pamper yourself for once. Just go upstairs and get your pajamas ready. I will be up in just a minute," Grandma said as she set our teacups on the counter by the sink and went off somewhere.

I went upstairs and selected a pair of pajama shorts, and a tank top and some fresh panties. Grandma came in, soon after, carrying a pouch of herbs.

"Try this, dear. Loop the strings over the faucet before you turn it on. As you draw your bath, the water will pour over the bag and make a relaxing tea bath," she said, handing me the pouch.

"I'm taking a bath in tea?" I said, sounding more disgusted than I had intended.

"There's some Epsom salt in here and rose petals, lavender and chamomile. It will be very relaxing and make your skin super soft. Trust me, dear, you will love it," Grandma said, pushing the bag into my hand.

I gave in and took a bath, and she was right. It really was so relaxing and smelled amazing. I forgot how stressed out I had been. When I went to my bedroom Grandma had put my new sheets and comforter on my bed, fresh out of the dryer. I felt so clean and relaxed as I drifted off to sleep, hugging Rocco's cheetah to my chest.

Chapter 13
GRACE

Ahead of time, I arranged for Meranda to get a ride to school with us for the school year. Emily's mother had been picking us up and driving us to school with her every day since seventh grade. She had to be to school early because she had cafeteria duty and we got to school early enough to eat breakfast there. Plus, it was nice to not have to walk or ride our bikes.

Emily's mother pulled up in her blue Dodge caravan. Emily, Bess, and Liv were already in the van. Meranda must have been watching for her because she came out of her house at the same time I came out of mine. Liv and Bess were sitting in the back and Emily was riding shotgun with her mother, so I climbed into the middle seat with Meranda sliding in behind me.

Emily's mother introduced herself. "Hi, Meranda. I'm Emily's mother. You can call me Mrs. Huddelson." She also told Meranda to let her know if she needed anything because she was married to the principal of the school.

The ride didn't last exceedingly long. We pulled up and parked in one of the reserved faculty spots closer to the school and got out. There were students standing in groups all around outside, wearing their new school clothes and shoes. A girl with her hair in a high blond bun ran over and told Mrs. Huddelson that she was excited to have her for World History. Walking into the school my stomach grumbled at the smell of sausage and maple. I assured Meranda that our school had delicious food and broke the stereotype of horrible cafeteria slop. She wouldn't regret eating at school every day with us.

Chapter 14

MERANDA

On the first day, I followed the girls through the breakfast line and put one of everything on my tray. One by one, each person typed in a number on a keypad and walked through the line to the cafeteria. When it was my turn, I didn't know what to do. I told the lady with the hair net working the register that I was new, and she asked for my name. She searched through a list of names and stopped near the end.

"Three-two-five-nine. Your account numba is three-two-five-nine. Every time you get a breakfast or lunch or even just a milk, you punch your numba into the keypad. Got it?" she said with a thick Boston accent.

"Yes, thank you," I said, humiliated. Everyone in line was staring at me.

"You can charge fah five days. If your parents don't pay, then you get a bagel fah breakfast and a peanut buttuh and jelly sandwich fah lunch," she said, waving me along.

After breakfast, I regretted my choice to eat. I was frazzled from the attention I got in the breakfast line and so nervous about going to my first class that the sausages and pancakes were churning in my stomach. The five of us walked up the stairs together to stop at our lockers. The day before, I had put a few things in mine; a magnetic mirror and a calendar, plus an extra brush. I didn't have a backpack or books yet and it wasn't cold enough for a jacket, so I wasn't planning to stop at mine.

Grace had a few things she wanted to leave in hers, so I walked with her to her locker. We noticed several people standing around mine, a crowd forming.

"What's going on?" I asked her.

"Your locker is next to Dean's. They are probably fawning over him," she said, just as Dean walked up behind us. "Oh, maybe not."

"Hey, what's going on?" Dean said, pushing his way through the crowd. As people backed away, we both saw it.

"Oh. My. Goddess!" Bess exclaimed from the other end of the hall.

"Who would do this? My dad is going to be furious!" Emily shouted. "Which one of you imbeciles did this?"

There was a picture taped to my locker and the words "FAT ASS" written in red. I stepped closer to get a better look. It was a picture printed on paper. Of me. Outside the school. My heart pounded super-fast, and the halls were chaos. I wasn't sure if I was going to scream or cry or have a heart attack. That's it. I was sure I was having a heart attack. Grace grabbed onto my shoulders and led me away. Emily told someone not to take it down so that her dad, the principal, could see.

Grace led me into an open room with a sink, an eye washing station, two cots and a small bathroom. Everything was a blur.

"I'm having a heart attack!" I said to the woman wearing navy blue nurse's scrubs.

"Her name is Meranda Wickstrom. She moved here from Hawaii, and this is her first day here. Someone vandalized her locker," Grace told the woman.

"You're kidding?! Meranda, I'm the school nurse. My name is Callie. Sit down right here. Can I have a listen to your heart?" She asked, putting a stethoscope on, and reaching the diaphragm out toward me.

I nodded and repeated that I was having a heart attack. After quickly examining me, she determined I wasn't having a heart attack.

"Sweetheart, have you ever had a panic attack before? It could feel like a heart attack if you never had one," she said, gently rubbing my back. The bell rang and Callie told Grace she better get to class.

After several minutes, there was a double beeping on the intercom and a voice came over the speaker.

"Welcome students. This is principal Huddelson. I have just a few quick announcements. First, there will be an assembly in the auditorium at nine o'clock to go over the rules in the student handbook. Students will be released to the auditorium by grade starting at 8:45. Also, it has come to my attention that one of the lockers in the tenth-grade wing has been vandalized. Anyone with information is asked to please come forward. Holy Orchard High takes bullying very seriously. You have one chance to come forward and receive a lesser punishment. If I have to check the cameras, the police will be involved. I will not tolerate bullying or vandalism in this school. Please work with me and the teachers to make this year a safe and happy one for *all* students. That is all. Thank you."

"Are you sure I'm not having a heart attack?" I asked the nurse.

"I'm sure. Do you want to try to calm down a little bit and see if you can make it for the assembly? Or would you rather I call your parents to come get you?" she asked.

I chose to have her call my grandma. Dad had found a job and started work the day before, plus I didn't want to deal with him. I was going to burst into tears at any moment and I wanted it to happen in a less public place.

Grandma was there to get me in less than fifteen minutes. She thanked Callie and escorted me out to the car. The moment she closed the passenger door for me, the waterworks came. The spasms in my diaphragm were jagged as I cried loud and hard.

Grandma said she would make me some calming tea and we could sit and talk, but suddenly she burst into tears, too. We sat in her car in front of the school and bawled our eyes out.

"Why are you crying?" I managed to ask her through my tears.

"I'm overwhelmed with sadness. I must be absorbing your emotions. It's extremely hard to see you cry like this and not be overcome myself. Can you calm down long enough so that I can drive us home, dear?"

When we got home, Grandma made me the tea she promised, and it worked at calming me down. It was almost like it was magic. She got a serious look on her face as she reached across the table and took my hand.

"Have you ever made anyone cry like that before?"

"What do you mean?" I asked, confused.

"When you cry hard, is everyone else usually crying?" She focused intently on me, waiting for an answer.

"Well, I guess any time I cry like that, something sad is happening or has happened so, yeah. I guess everyone is usually crying when I am crying hard. Why are you asking me this? I am confused, Grandma."

Grandma squeezed my hand and said, "We need to have a talk."

Chapter 15

MERANDA

Grandma refilled my tea, then went back to holding my hand. She asked me to not repeat anything to my dad that she was about to tell me, that he wouldn't understand, and he would keep me from her again. I got really scared as Grandma's tone was serious. I promised I wouldn't tell him, then she took in a deep breath.

"I don't know how else to tell you this, but you are a witch. I am a witch. We come from a long line of witches," Grandma paused to gauge my reaction.

"Ha-ha, very funny. What do you really need to tell me?"

Grandma's eyebrows lowered, and the corners of her mouth turned downward.

"Oh, you are serious?" I said aloud. My Grandma was a crazy person.

"We are witches. I bet you can sense other people's emotions. We are empaths," she said, raising her eyebrows as if trying to determine if she had convinced me. I was sure I still appeared confused and unbelieving because she continued. "We have special abilities, and all witches are bonded to a certain element. Mine is earth element. I can make things grow," she said, waving her hand across the room toward the many house plants scattered throughout.

"Oh, uh. Oh," I said, trying to grasp what she was saying to me. I could tell she was telling me the truth, or she at least believed she was.

"I wasn't sure, but I always guessed your element was water. I found your social media account online, and you were always around water in your pictures. Sailing, surfing, snorkeling, swimming. Then there was the accident, and you survived. I think your bond to water helped keep you from drowning that day," Grandma said, reaching for me with shaking hands. I pushed against the table with my hands to back out of my chair.

"How could you say that? That my mom and Rocco died, and *I* didn't because... Because why? Because I'm a witch? Because I'm bonded to the water element, and it didn't let me die? That I have some power that could save me from drowning, yet I wouldn't use it to save my *family*?!"

I was about to storm off when Grandma slammed her fist on the table in anger. "Meranda, you are a witch!"

She must have seen the hurt in my eyes because she instantly begged my forgiveness. "I'm so sorry, dear. That is what I am trying to tell you. All witches are empaths to some extent. It's rare, but some can control other people's emotions. Your emotions are so strong, and you haven't learned how to control your power. Your emotions are overpowering mine." Grandma came toward me, and I put my hands up.

"No. Stop. I am going upstairs. I won't tell Dad about this, but I want you to leave me alone," I demanded. Then, I went up to my room. I needed to be alone to think. I wasn't sure if I was considering the possibility that what she just told me was true. I couldn't wrap my head around it.

Chapter 16
GRACE

I sat next to Emily, Bess, and Liv at the assembly. Meranda wasn't anywhere around, and we assumed that she was either still in the nurse's office or she went home. Emily told us that "FAT ASS" was written in permanent red marker and whoever took the photo did so the day before, when we were at the open house. Poor Meranda. She was humiliated. I would have been, too, if it were me. How were we going to convince Meranda to stay in Holy Orchard and join our coven if someone was bullying her on the first day?

On the ride home, Mrs. Huddelson told us that Mr. Huddelson checked the cameras and a large insect climbed up on the lens of the camera facing Meranda's locker, moments before the culprit vandalized her locked. Once the lens was clear, the person was already gone, and the damage already done. The only way to find out who it was would be if they confessed. My guess was that wasn't going to happen. Mr. Huddelson said the police would be involved. I wondered if they would take fingerprints, but Emily said they wouldn't waste their time because hundreds of people, students, the custodians, even teachers at some point may have touched that locker.

When I got home from school, I immediately texted Meranda to find out if she wanted to get together. I offered to tell her all about our teachers and the first day. She wasn't interested. This was the first day since I met her that she didn't want to hang out. I couldn't blame her, though, after the rotten first day she had. She assured me that she just needed some time to herself and that she would give Holy Orchard High another try tomorrow. I composed a text promising we would find out who did this, then I set my phone on my nightstand and greeted Tinkerbell, who was already mewing for me in the pet carrier.

My mother came home at lunch and fed Tinkerbell for me, and she was already hungry again. I made a bottle of kitten milk replacer and sat on my bed feeding and stroking her. How could anyone be so cruel to someone they don't even know? Who could have vandalized her locker? And so viciously. It was directed toward Meranda because there was a picture of *her*. Someone was watching her. Maybe even watching *all of us*. Goosebumps pricked the surface of the skin on my arms as chilling air wrapped around me.

There weren't many people who even knew who Meranda was. Only some of the faculty, her family and us. But I didn't think any one of us could be involved in such a cruel act. Maybe someone was targeting the coven and Meranda just happened to be with us. I shivered at the thought. Was the coven the intended target?

Chapter 17
MERANDA

I stormed out of the kitchen and stomped up the stairs like a child. I hadn't acted like that in years. *Who does this woman think she is??* I was so angry that Grandma would even suggest such nonsense. After everything I'd been through in the previous weeks. My *Kapuna* would never have said such things to me.

I was so angry that tears poured from my eyes like a dam had broken inside me. As hard as I tried, I couldn't stop them from flowing. I stood in the middle of my room with my hands balled into fists, my jaw clenched and every muscle in my body tightening. I threw myself onto my bed and punched my pillow as hard as I could, but nothing I did could stop the tears from coming. So, I let go.

I cried long and hard. I was sure Grandma could hear me, but she did as I asked and stayed away. The last time I cried this hard was the day of the funeral. I finally calmed down and my tears had run out. All that was left was the little hiccup that came from my diaphragm every few seconds.

I wanted to text Leilani, back home, and tell her how crazy my grandma is, but Hawaii is 6 hours behind Massachusetts. Leilani would have been in school. I hugged the pillow I had punched as if I were sorry for hurting it. I breathed deeply, the scent of Grandma's lavender laundry soap and my eyes were suddenly too heavy to keep open. I thought of Mom and Rocco, and the day of the accident. How did I get out of the water? When I was searching the water, after finding Rocco's empty life vest, something had hit me in the head and I blacked out. Why couldn't I remember?

I must have fallen asleep because I was suddenly dreaming. I've had lots of dreams like this. So vivid. Everything was super clear and focused. It felt like reality, but I wasn't me. Who was I?

I was a woman, wearing a dress like the mannequins in the Holy Orchard History Museum. The 1600s I guessed. My hair was long and blond, and I had fair skin, the opposite of what I really looked like.

I sat up in bed scanning the room. I was in some sort of rustic cabin or old home. There was a small wooden table and a chair across the room with a wicker basket of apples on top of it. I was afraid.

I listened carefully, the sound of hooves hit the dirt, got louder and louder, then came to a stop outside. I stood up, grabbed a white bonnet from a hook, pulled it on my head and tied it under my chin. The door burst open, and panic invaded my chest. I screamed, but my voice wasn't my own. Three men pushed their way in. A man with glasses and a mustache, wearing a faded brown suit, grabbed my right arm. I tried to pull away as another man, wearing a hat and what appeared to be a pilgrim's costume, grabbed my other arm. The third man approached me with a menacing grin. He had a brown beard only a couple of inches below his chin, with silver hairs throughout.

"What is the meaning of this?" I asked, my voice shaking as the men tightened their grips on me.

"*Elizabeth Ferris, you are accused of witchcraft. Your resistance is futile. You shall be tried in front of the town in one fortnight,*" the man announced.

"*Where are you taking me?*" I asked, but no answer was given. The men bound my hands and took me away on a horse. My arms tingled and the numbness grew in my fingers. My heart was beating nearly out of my chest. A panic attack, not a heart attack, I had learned recently.

Time passed in slow motion. What kind of dream was this? I've dreamed I was other people before, but nothing like this. I could feel everything. I could taste my morning breath, feel the ropes digging into my wrists, smell the horse poop.

We arrived at a stone building with bars on the windows. It was small. The floor was dirt and there were six cells, three on each side with two rows facing each other. All the cells were unoccupied from what I could see. I was pulled off the horse by one of the men and dragged toward the first cell. I was no longer fighting, and it took the man almost no effort to carry me.

The man with the beard took out a rusty key and unlocked the cell door. Once I was closer, I got a better glimpse of how small this cell was. It was inhumane. There was only standing room. Someone shoved me hard into the cell and my shoulder hit the stone wall. I felt the sharp pain like it was really happening to me. The man with the beard shut the door and locked it.

"*Surely this is a mistake, Sir. I am no witch. Please? I've been on my feet all day picking apples from the orchard,*" I cried as the man ignored my pleas and walked away from me. "*Is it not possible to lay down or even sit to rest my feet?*" My pleading was pointless because the men paid me no attention.

Pounding hooves in the distance came closer again. The man with the beard returned with the key and I thought he was going to let me out, but the hooves got louder. More men were coming in on horses, carrying another blond-haired woman with her hands bound. She stared up at me and smiled.

"*Grandma?*" *I shouted, confused. Nobody could hear me. The woman was my grandma. She appeared younger, but it was her. I was sure of it. They pushed her into the cell across from me and the man with the beard locked the door.*

Grandma reached her arm through the bars to the man with the beard and caressed his cheek. He turned and grabbed her hand, "Don't touch me, WITCH!"

"Are you afraid you will fall in love with me, Mayor Wickstrom?" she cooed. I'd never seen my grandma like this. It was terrifying.

The mayor pulled away from Grandma and said, "Sarah Sutton, you will be hanged!"

"Sarah Sutton?" I asked aloud.

"Yes, Dear," she said, smiling.

"Oh, I thought you were someone else. You look like someone I know," I said as I rubbed the bruise forming on my shoulder.

"But I am. You only exist because of me," she said, using her fingernails to pick something out of her teeth.

"What?" I asked. "Grandma?"

"Yes, Dear?"

I opened my eyes and Grandma was standing in my doorway. I thought I shut that.

"You were calling for me," she said, her eyes shining like she had been crying.

"No, I wasn't. I was sleeping," I said in a tone like I was ready for another fight.

"Meranda, how about you come downstairs. I made beef stew and blueberry muffins for dessert. Let's talk about your dream."

I noticed the clock on my nightstand. It was nearly 8 PM. "Is Dad home?"

"He is catching up with an old buddy from high school. Turns out he's one of your dad's new co-workers. I told him it would be lovely if they went out for a drink." Grandma opened the door wider and motioned for me to follow. I didn't want to follow, but I missed lunch and dinner, and my stomach was growling.

Grandma sat across from me at the table and watched me as she sipped her tea. I ate two bowls of beef stew and took a small bite of a blueberry muffin before she spoke.

"Sarah Sutton is our ancestor. The first known Wickstrom witch," Grandma said, breaking the silence.

I nearly choked on my muffin as I gasped mid-swallow, "What?"

"You are angry at me. You think I am crazy. But I'm not. Hear me out?" Grandma said, her eyes pleading me.

"Sarah Sutton was the servant of the first mayor of Holy Orchard. His name was Eli Wickstrom. Our ancestor. During the witch trials, Sarah was accused and found guilty. She was set to be hanged. But she was found dead in her cell the morning she was scheduled to be hanged," Grandma said, stopping to take a sip of her tea.

"You are scaring me, Grandma. I didn't tell you anything about my dream," I said, touching the goosebumps that covered my arms. My fingers barely caressed my shoulder and I flinched from the pain of a new bruise. Where my shoulder had hit the stone wall in my dream.

Grandma must have realized my discovery because she said she was sorry I got hurt.

"But how?" I asked.

"I am a witch, Dear. One of my abilities is to send people dreams. I can enter them and control them. They are real as if they are actually happening in that moment. People can get hurt in these kinds of dreams. Die even," she said reaching across the table for my hand.

I didn't know what to do, what to think. I was in shock, but I needed the comfort, so I let Grandma take my hand. I said nothing and let her continue.

"I've been sending you dreams since you were little. Have you wondered why I was so familiar to you when we met? It's because I would visit you in your dreams every night when you were younger. I stopped when you got a little older because I was afraid you would understand what was going on. Remember Roger the gnome?"

"Roger? That was you?" I asked, my heart raced for the third time that day.

"No, silly. I was me. Don't you remember? Roger was a friend we created together."

It all hit me at once. I remembered Roger, the goofy gnome I used to dream of all the time when I was a kid. We would go on so many adventures in the woods, in the mountains, so many places I'd never been to in real life. I remembered her. The blond-haired woman who always showed up in my dreams. I forgot about her until that moment. I could always smell her, the lavender. I told my mom about her before, and she said I watched too much TV. I wasn't allowed to watch TV as much after that.

"This can't be happening." I said abandoning my half-eaten muffin.

"It is. It's real. Let me prove it."

Chapter 18
GRACE

The second day of school wasn't nearly as dramatic as the first. Everyone had forgotten about Meranda's vandalized locker, but she was quiet the whole day. Until P.E. last hour. All of us had P.E. together except Liv. Since Meranda missed the first day, she wasn't there to get first dibs on the gym uniforms. All that was left were XLs. She was drowning in her uniform and Mr. Ritter told her she would have to wait a week until the new order of smaller sizes came in.

We counted off by two's and were put on teams for kickball. Meranda and I were on the same team, while Emily and Bess were on the other. I was excited to be on Meranda's team. She was very athletic, and I wanted to make sure she was doing okay after what happened. Our team was up to kick, and I was chosen to go first. Naturally, I kicked the ball straight to Allison Bymark and she jumped to catch it, her too tight gym uniform riding up slightly to expose her belly button. I momentarily thought about the fact that she and Meranda should trade gym uniforms, as I walked to the bleachers because I was out. Some of the boys snickered and pointed as I took my seat and I laughed back in a mocking tone.

Meranda was up next to kick. She tightened the drawstrings on her gym shorts and tied them in a bow, then she made her stance, ready to kick the ball. Allison rolled the ball toward her with a smirk on her face. Meranda pulled her right leg back behind her to build up momentum then kicked forward; her foot made contact with the ball. It shot forward and flew fast, inches away from Allison's face, and kept going. It was good! As the other team, including Bess and Emily, scrambled to get hold of the ball that landed somewhere in the bleachers, Meranda ran her bases. Our team cheered and clapped loudly.

"WOOO! Go Meranda!!" I yelled, excitedly. Finally, something good was happening. I took my eyes off her for only a second when there was a *SMACK* and a mixture of screams and laughter. Meranda was on the ground and her shorts were at her ankles, her underwear exposed for all to see. I ran to her as fast as I could, but Emily and Bess were already helping her up. She appeared stunned as Emily and Bess struggled to pull her shorts back up. Her knees and chin were scraped from rubbing against the floor when she fell.

"That's enough!" Mr. Ritter yelled at the students who were laughing. "Walk it off," he said to Meranda. "Go get a drink and regain your composure," he said, lowering his voice as he directed Bess to go with her. The game continued and the next person in line went up to kick.

Chapter 19
MERANDA

B ess looped her arm around mine and walked with me through the door of the gymnasium, into the hallway. My chin and knees ached and stung. I couldn't let myself cry, as much as I wanted to.

"I tied my shorts tight. They shouldn't have fallen," I said, taking a deep breath as Bess led me to the drinking fountain.

"You tied them. That was weird. Maybe you're cursed. Maybe...," she said, then she paused. I got the impression she stopped herself from saying something she wasn't supposed to say. Bess shrugged her shoulders. "I can walk you to the nurse's office and tell Mr. Ritter your knees are bleeding. I'm sure he wouldn't mind."

"Is every day going to be filled with embarrassment? They saw my underwear. All of them," I said, remembering the words on my locker the day before. *Fat Ass.*

"Sometimes high school really sucks, but I think it will get better. And no matter what anyone thinks in this school, you still have at least five friends," she said, her cherry glossed lips curving into a hopeful smile.

"Five?"

"Me, Emily, Grace, Liv and Dean," she said, confidently.

"Dean is my cousin. He's not my friend," I said.

"Actually, Dean was really worried about you yesterday and I think you should recognize that he is one of your strongest supporters at this school. He is also super powerful and it's a good thing that he is on your side. Cousin or not," she said, as I bent forward and took a long drink out of the fountain.

"I just met him. I didn't even know he existed until I got here," I said, trying to argue, though I wasn't sure why.

"You also just met the rest of us. You didn't know any of us until you got here, but we love you already. Can't you feel that connection?" She stared deep into my eyes like she was trying to reach my soul. My grandma's voice spoke in my head and reminded me about being a witch and an empath. I focused on Bess, sure I could feel her heart skipping and I could sense warmth and love coming from her. She was telling the truth.

"Also, what do you mean he is super powerful?" I asked.

"Just that he is so popular in the school and his opinions matter to a lot of people. If he is on your side, everyone else will be, too," she said, hugging my waist, "soon enough anyway. I'm sure of it."

Somehow, I avoided having a panic attack. I was embarrassed, but Bess calmed me with her words. Maybe I *was* a witch, or at least an empath. I declined the walk to the nurse's office and chose to go back to the gym. The game was over, and our team had won, according to the score board overhead. The class was running laps around the gym.

"Two more laps, then you can go get changed. When you are done, wait for the bell by the door. See you tomorrow," Mr. Ritter announced to the class. He excused me to go get dressed but sent Bess to run her laps.

<hr />

The locker room had two walls lined with small lockers, six high. They looked like cages. Some had pad locks on them. Some were empty. Each row of lockers had long benches in front of them. I sat down on the bench in front of the locker I had chosen to put my clothes in at the start of class. I didn't have a padlock. As I untied my gym shoes, there was a shuffling noise that came from behind me. The wall at my back had rows of sinks and two large mirrors, with a divider wall between them. There were four hand dryers.

There didn't appear to be anyone in the room with me, but I glanced around. Beyond the doorway to the shower room was darkness. The lights were off, but I suddenly felt a tingle go up my back and my hair stood on end like I was being watched. Holding my breath, I stayed silent for several moments, but there wasn't another sound. I turned back to my locker as I kicked off my gym shoes. I pulled my clothes and shoes out of the locker. There was something wet on my hands. When I pulled them out my hands were covered in ink. I examined my clothes and found an exploded ink pen in the middle. Black ink was spilled across my t-shirt, jeans and even on my white shoes.

Rolling the pen in my fingers, I noticed the familiar mermaid design from the stationary set I bought for school. It was *my* pen, but I didn't remember having it with me. Thinking of what Bess said in the hallway, I spoke aloud, "Maybe I *am* cursed." Suddenly, the door from the gym creaked open and a herd of teenage girls came rushing in.

Grace, Emily, and Bess sat down on the bench near me and pulled their things out of their lockers. Grace noticed my damaged clothing first and gasped. Emily and Bess looked, first at my face then at my clothes.

"How did that happen?" Grace asked.

"Do you believe in witches?" I whispered.

All three of them stared at me with raised eyebrows, but I could sense something from all of them. What was it? I couldn't tell. I could sense their hearts beating faster. They seemed afraid, but excited. Both? I glared at them and raised my eyebrows, without speaking, as if to prompt them to answer me. Grace finally answered as the bell rang and our classmates filed out of the room.

"Let's meet at my house. We should talk about this," she said, looking at Bess and Emily, as if giving them a silent invitation to attend.

Chapter 20
GRACE

Pulling my backpack from my locker, I quickly filled it with books, then I rushed over to find Liv at her locker. She was looking through her history notes and gave me a fake smile.

"We are meeting at my house. Coven meeting," I said. Liv nodded, tossing the last of her books into her school bag and slung her gym bag over her shoulder. We walked together quickly to meet the rest of the girls outside, but Liv didn't seem to have anything to say.

Waiting at Mrs. Huddelson's car in the parking lot, Emily's phone chimed of an incoming text. She was silent for a few seconds then looked up at us.

"Well, this sucks," she said, clicking her tongue and putting her free hand on her hip. "Mom said she had an unexpected meeting with a parent come up, so... we can either wait who-knows how long for her to be done, or we can take the bus," Emily said, looking to me for direction.

"OK..." I tried to think hard and fast, just as the bus to my house pulled away from the curb. I turned to the girls with my best fake smile and asked, "Who's up for walking?"

In awkward silence we walked, and I was deep in thought, trying to figure out how I would say what I wanted to say. I was unsure of what information Meranda had. I wondered if her grandmother told her anything, or everything. I understood what she was getting at, when she asked if I believed in witches, moments after I noticed the ink spilled all over her clothes. She was wondering if I believed a witch was responsible.

In Holy Orchard there were a lot of wannabe witches because of the history of our town. Some really were witches with abilities like empathy, green magic and spell work, but we were the only ones in town, as far as I was aware, who had powers enough to curse someone. And we were still learning.

When we arrived at my house, Meranda ran to drop off her things at her house and change out of her gym uniform, since she was right next door. That gave me a few minutes to talk privately with the coven.

"What does she know?" Emily asked.

"I can't be sure. She hasn't said anything to make me think she knows. Her grandmother told me she lived a very sheltered life and witchcraft was kept from her," I said, pacing the room. "We needed to let her find out on her own or she would have been scared off. As soon as I saw her that first day, I recognized it was her. She is our missing witch. But I think she believes a witch has cursed her," I paused momentarily, deep in thought. "We must find out what she knows without scaring her off. I just don't know how to do that," I glanced over at Bess, and she had a guilty look on her face. "What?"

"Maybe she doesn't know, because..."

"Because why?" I asked.

"Well after she fell and we went to get a drink, I said something," Bess raised her brows and clenched her cheek. She was hesitating too long.

"Spill it out, Bess!" Emily said sternly.

"I said she might be cursed. Then I considered what I said and changed the subject. It was right after that she found her clothes in the locker room."

"OK, I am so lost right now," Liv said, prompting us to tell the story of gym class.

We told Liv the story and finished just in time for Meranda to come in the front door and up the stairs to my room. By then, we were sitting cross-legged on the rug in the center of my room, and I was holding my kitten Tinkerbell. Meranda came in, shut the door behind her and sat on the floor between me and Bess.

"So, why'd my question about witches initiate a meeting at your house?" she asked.

I adjusted myself on the floor and continued to stroke Tinkerbell. Bess coughed, prompting me to answer.

"Well, would you care to elaborate what you meant when you asked if I believed in witches?"

Meranda thought for a second and opened her mouth to talk, but she didn't say anything. She took a breath and started again.

"My grandma told me I'm a witch. That I have powers. That I am an empath and more," she said putting her left hand to her forehead like it ached. "That I will get stronger as I learn and come into my powers more. She is crazy! Right? Witches don't exist," she paused as if waiting for someone else to say something, but nobody spoke. "Actually, I don't know. Maybe she's not. A lot of things in my life don't add up right now."

"Tell her," Emily said, kicking my foot. Everyone, including Meranda, stared at me, waiting for my response.

I was torn. I desperately wanted to tell her everything about us, about our powers, about meeting the fortune teller at the county fair, and our spell to call a lost witch exactly two weeks before she showed up. I also believed whole-heartedly that she was our lost witch, and I didn't want to scare her away, but she was looking at me. They were *all* looking at me, then at her. Meranda's eyes never left mine.

"Witches are real," Bess said softly, looking away from me to Meranda. "We are all witches. I bet your grandma isn't crazy."

"We are a coven... of witches," I added, suddenly less nervous. There was another awkward silence and Meranda didn't respond.

"We have powers. We put spells on people and sacrifice animals," Liv said, with her eyebrows lowered.

"Liv, what the Hell?! We do *not* do those things, why would you say that?" I said in disbelief.

"Well, why are you all tip-toeing around and acting *so* scared to say anything? This is who we are and if she is destined to join our coven, she won't be scared off, "Liv said, standing up to leave. "If she is scared off that easy then maybe she doesn't belong here. Why did we waste our time on a spell to call a lost witch? Anyway, I don't have time for this. My shift starts in 45 minutes. See you later."

Liv rushed out the door without looking back and her heavy footsteps boomed down the stairs and out the front door.

"WOW! Who pooped in her cornflakes this morning?" Bess asked. Then everyone turned and stared at me.

"I'm not sure what her problem is, but please don't let her scare you off. We would never sacrifice animals. We love animals. We did do a spell to call a lost witch. We are missing our 5th and we believe you are her," I said, hopeful that she would be receptive.

"So, say I believe you? What sort of powers do we all have? Can we fly on broomsticks? Turn people into frogs? Shoot fire out of our fingertips?" Meranda asked, wiggling her fingers in the air. "Because that would be awesome."

"Well, it isn't like that. There's magic, but there are rules. We have a Book of Shadows, and we can do spell work. We can make things happen, but we only do good. We don't want to hurt anyone. My grandmother said anything we do comes back on us three-fold," I said, putting Tink on the floor, letting her wander the room.

"So, we don't really have powers? We can't fly. Can't turn our exes into toads?"

"Not really. At least, I don't think so. But we can sense things. We are all empaths to varying degrees. I can make things grow with no effort and nurse plants and animals back to health. My element is earth. Liv can kind of manipulate the weather. She can also stay in the water for long periods of time. Her element is water," I said.

"If anyone would be able to fly... it would be me," Bess started, "my element is air. I can also kind of manipulate the weather. I can call wind, but I'm not super strong yet. I can also use the air to eaves drop on conversations and send rotten smells to people like Allison Bymark."

"My element is fire. I can burn things," Emily said seriously, then laughed. "Well, I can't exactly ignite things on fire. I've tried but it just goes out. Maybe when I get stronger, I might possibly be able to do that. I can ignite a flame on a candle, and I've been practicing small campfires. I can also read flames. I can see people and things inside flames when I concentrate. I am still trying to learn how to actually read what they mean, though."

Meranda seemed to consider what we were telling her. She appeared to be a little confused, then she inhaled deeply, concentrating on each of us.

"OK, so you are earth element," she said pointing to me, "you are air," she pointed to Bess, "you are fire," she pointed to Emily, "and Liv is water? So, what other element is there, then?"

"It depends on who you ask. To some, they only recognize earth, air, wind, and fire, but for some there is a fifth element. Spirit," I said, getting up to sit on my bed.

"Spirit? Then I don't think I have a place in your coven. My grandma said I have an affinity to the water element. I practically lived in the water in Hawaii," she paused, thinking. "My family died in that accident. I should have died, too, but my grandma said it was my affinity to the water element that made me survive. If you already have a water element, then I'm not your girl. Right?"

Bess reached over to touch Meranda's hand, and she shoved it away, getting up.

"That would be, if I believed any of this, which I don't. So... How about you all just leave me alone!"

And like that she was gone. She stormed out of my room faster than Liv had. I texted her multiple times. We all had, but she only responded to say she didn't need a ride to school the next day. I was sure, at that moment, that we blew it.

Chapter 21
MERANDA

L aying on my bed, I considered the events of the entire day. I had stormed out of Grace's house and into my grandma's house. *My house.* Grandma kept her distance because I was upset... again. Thinking of the possibility that I could be a witch, that I had powers that saved me, but not my family, in the accident. The thought of having friends and belonging, only to find out that I wasn't what they were looking for. Spirit. What did it even mean really? Maybe Grandma was wrong. Maybe my affinity wasn't with the water element. Maybe I didn't selfishly save myself and let my family die. I should have asked Grace what someone with an affinity to the spirit element might be able to do, but it was too late. I embarrassed myself, yet again.

I didn't even read the twelve messages I had received from Grace, Emily, and Bess. I tapped the top one from Grace and replied to say I wouldn't need a ride to school in the morning. With how I acted, it made sense to punish myself by walking.

What did I get myself into? I had to get up an hour early to walk and it was freezing outside. My breath was a visible cloud in front of me and my sweatshirt was not cutting it. Grandma wasn't kidding me when she said I would need to buy a warmer jacket. I couldn't remember the last time I had been that cold. Had I ever been that cold? Suddenly, my vision became clouded, and it felt like I was in water.

My head was throbbing with a sharp pain. I was sure it was bleeding, but I was under water. I wasn't sure how deep I was, but I was sinking fast. My arms and legs were paralyzed with the realization that my family was dead, and I couldn't hold my breath much longer. I kept the record at my school for longest time holding my breath. I used to practice for hours every day with Leilani. We would hold our breath until we felt like passing out. This was it, I was dying, but it didn't matter anyway. I had nothing to live for. My mom and Rocco were dead.

My lungs burned. It felt like my head was going to explode. I tried, but I couldn't hold my breath anymore. I felt the invisible vice grip squeezing my brain. I couldn't do it. The release came as I inhaled, and water flooded into my lungs. My nasal passage burned, water flowing through. My life flashed before my eyes. Mom and Dad on the beach, teaching me to surf, back when they used to spend time together. Rocco, emerging from Mom's birthing pool as she held him out, having just delivered him herself. Dad, a single tear in his eye. Did he cry when I was born? Leilani, when she held my face after the luau, the first time she kissed me... I accepted my fate, ready to die, but then I was breathing... under water.

I stepped down from the curb, nearly rolling my ankle.

WITCHES OF HOLY ORCHARD

"What the HELL was that?!" I said out loud. It was a memory. The chirp on my watch alerted me it was 8:00. I was late for school. When I looked at my watch in a panic, the time read 9:00. There was no way! I was sure that my watch was off an hour, so I pulled out my cell phone and checked the time. My phone said 9:01 AM. It was incomprehensible. How? I had flashbacks before, but I never lost time. I lost over an hour. Remembering how cold I was, I walked faster down the street. Unsure of how I would explain my tardiness, I stopped at the corner. Hugging my arms, I tried to stay warm.

They'd never believe I "lost" time. I'd most likely get detention, and everyone would stare at me when I walked in. Holy Orchard High was like a nightmare. Not just the school. The town of Holy Orchard, period. I wished I could fly home and throw myself into Leilani's arms. I missed her so much, but we hardly talked since I got to Holy Orchard. The last time we talked, she said it was too painful to hear my voice and know she couldn't touch me. Maybe out of sight, out of mind was easier for her, but it wasn't for me. I was hurt, but the anger was rising in me.

My feelings were all over the place. Anger. Sadness. Grief. Fear. Confusion. For the first time, I needed my grandma. Instead of crossing the street toward Holy Orchard High, I turned down the block and headed home. As much as I hated it, Holy Orchard... Grandma's house... It was my home, and I needed it.

Chapter 22
GRACE

When Meranda didn't show up for school, Liv said we should stop wasting our time on her. If she didn't want us, then we didn't need her. We were wasting a lot of time and energy on someone who wasn't interested. Bess and Emily didn't want to give up. The three of us tried texting Meranda, throughout the day, but we never got a response. We discussed it as a group and agreed that Liv was right, although she was happier about it than we were. We needed to focus on practicing our witchcraft, learning more spells, and trying to grow in our powers. If Meranda was our lost witch, she would find her way to us. If not, then we wouldn't be any worse off than we were before she showed up.

Chapter 23
MERANDA

Bursting through the front door of my new Victorian home, I yelled out frantically for Grandma. She had planned to go shopping in Boston and my only hope, in that moment, was that she hadn't left yet.

"Grandma!" I yelled. Tears streaked my face as I cried. "Grandma!" Heavy footsteps rushed from somewhere in the house and Grandma emerged from the library.

"What's the matter? What is it?" Grandma asked, reaching for me as I fell into her arms, sobbing.

Momentarily, I felt like I was being held by my mom again. I missed her. I needed her. Then I remembered the painful feeling of drowning and the realization that I could breathe under water.

"Grandma," I whispered, staring up into her eyes, "I can breathe under water."

Grandma squeezed me tight and rubbed my back. She didn't say anything right away, but I could *feel* her heartbeat. It was racing at first but slowed to a comfortable pace as I calmed down.

"You feel that Dear? You are learning to control it." She said, pulling back and holding me at arms' length.

"Controlling what?" I asked, lowering my eyebrows.

"You ran in here all upset, crying hysterically. You gave me such a fright. I thought there would be a repeat of the other day where you would turn me into a sobbing mess. But you are learning to control your emotions," Grandma hugged me again, then continued. "Your power is extraordinarily strong, and you could use it to do such good. You may even make a career out of it one day."

"What are you talking about Grandma? I am so confused right now," I cried again.

"Your empathy. All witches are empathetic. Remember? But you have the rare ability to control other people's emotions. When you first got here you were making everyone feel what you were feeling, but you are gaining control of it. I am so proud of you!"

I listened for Grandma's heartbeat and let is calm me down again. Getting sidetracked, I asked her how I could make a career out of that.

"My dear, you would be able to calm individuals or large groups of people. You would make a great nurse, or even one of those jobs with the police de-escalating situations," Grandma considered her words then continued, "of course, your powers could be used for manipulation. To get what you want. You could be a lawyer or a politician. You could really help people, but... on the other hand, you could hurt people. Use their emotions to control them and situations around you, but that wouldn't be right, and I trust that you would only use your powers for good. You are a Wickstrom, and *we* are good."

Grandma took my hand and led me to the kitchen. She already had a pot of tea ready, like she knew I would be home soon. As she poured us both a cup of chamomile lavender tea, she smiled at me.

"So, what is it you were saying about breathing under water?" she asked.

"Grandma, something happened on the way to school. I blacked out and lost time," the tears fought to push their way out again. "I had a memory of the accident. Mom and Rocco were dead and..." I was getting choked up remembering it. "I was drowning, Grandma. I could feel it. I was dying. But then I inhaled, and I could breathe under water."

I looked at Grandma, trying to gauge her reaction. She was silent and deep in thought. I could sense her heartbeat speeding up. She was keeping something from me. My own heart pounded inside my chest as the anger built up inside me.

"Grandma?" I asked, sternly.

"That's how you survived. I suspected one of two things. You could either part the seas or breathe under water. You would have amazing powers either way," Grandma said, sipping her tea.

"How could you know? Are you psychic?" I asked, genuinely wanting to understand.

"Me? Psychic? No..." Grandma giggled, remembering something. "I had a friend once who was psychic. She predicted that I would have a granddaughter who would be immensely powerful. I was blessed with a troop of grandsons. The Wickstrom men rarely have any magical abilities at all." Grandma smiled and sipped her tea again. "My Nathan would have a daughter. There was always something about him. He was embarrassed and ashamed. He shied away from anything to do with magic. Your aunts embraced it. They wished for daughters, and it just didn't happen. But Nathan... he pretended magic didn't exist. He would be the one to give me a powerful granddaughter. That is just the way the world works most of the time. I was certain he'd have twin girls. Maybe even triplets."

AMY SOUTHARD

Time flew by as I visited with Grandma in the kitchen. She told me stories of my dad and aunts growing up. She made me forget the trauma of the day briefly, until the house phone rang. It was my school. Grandma told them I was ill today, and she simply forgot to call and tell them I wouldn't be there. She told them I probably would need to miss tomorrow, too, but I should be good as new by Monday.

Grandma sat back down at the table and said, "You got to try to not miss any more school. If you miss too many days, they make you repeat the grade. But I bought you an extra day to get over your *illness*." Grandma laughed and it was contagious. I laughed, too. Two witches, laughing in the kitchen. It was nice.

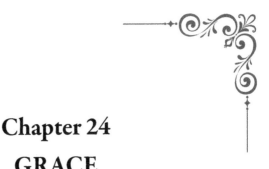

Chapter 24
GRACE

Even though we backed off Meranda, I couldn't help but be concerned that she wasn't in school on Thursday or Friday. Her grandmother tended to the mums in the backyard and her father left for work as usual. I was sure Meranda was OK, but I lost a good friend. We made the decision, as a coven, to focus on magic and strengthening our powers. We couldn't focus on our missing fifth and Liv was technically right. If it was truly destined for us to have a fifth and if Meranda was that person, then it would happen in time anyway, whether we did anything or not.

Liv, Emily, and Bess stayed the night at my house on Friday and we spent the evening practicing spell work from my Book of Shadows. The book was an old, handmade journal that belonged to my grandmother. She had stretched the leather and bound the book herself. The text was handwritten, and the artwork was beautiful. There were spells for all kinds of things. *Clearing up acne.* That was the first spell we tried. Bess and Emily already had near perfect skin, but Liv and I had a few pimples to get rid of. The spell called for moon water. Thankfully, we had some moon water left over from a spell we did a couple weeks earlier. Many of Grandmother's spells called for moon water.

Moon Water

1. Choose a vessel, such as a glass jar or bottle and set your intentions. Make sure the vessel has a cap or lid to keep bugs and debris from entering the moon water.

2. Surround the jar with crystals. Any crystal will do, but black tourmaline will absorb threatening energy. Fluorite will create openness and clarity.

3. Place the vessel outside, if possible, on the night of a full moon. Near a window will suffice in a pinch, if the window allows moonlight to shine through.

4. Leave the jar out for 24 hours, or overnight if needed right away.

5. Retrieve your charged moon water and use in your favorite spells.

Note: Do not drink unless water source was clean prior to charging and cap was in place.

The last part was written in a different ink and the handwriting was a little sloppier, as if it were added many years later. Maybe Grandmother had personal experience with that.

The spell for clearing up acne did not have instant results. That was a little disappointing for Liv, but I had faith in it. We were instructed to set our intentions. Then we were to wash our faces *or other areas* with the moon water, close our eyes and imagine the moon water washing out the impurities and the acne clearing up. I squirted a few medicine droppers full of moon water into a shallow dish and Liv and I dipped our cloth make-up pads into it, rubbing them over our faces like toner. We closed our eyes and imagined our acne clearing up. Emily and Bess did this part, too, even though they had nothing to clear up.

When we opened our eyes, we examined ourselves in the mirror and nothing was different, although I swore I felt something tingle under my skin. Liv grumbled and said she believed my moon water was tainted.

When we woke up in the morning, both of our faces were perfectly clear. There wasn't a single pimple on either one of us. Liv was ecstatic. Emily had the start of a new pimple, so we repeated the spell for Emily and Bess, just to be safe.

We took turns flipping through the Book of Shadows. It contained hundreds of spells. We briefly joked about how it was called a *Book of Shadows*, but there was nothing dark in it whatsoever. *Finding your spirit animal, Calling your familiar, Cure for a broken heart*. I used that one last year when my father passed away. I think it helped.

There were recipes for *Good Luck Cake, Merry Party Punch, Confidence Cookies,* and *Inspiration Tea*. Liv had to work at the cafe then had swim team practice after. When she got back to my house Saturday night, she was insistent that we make the Good Luck Cake.

"They will be choosing team captain next weekend. I'm sure I'm guaranteed to get it, but just as a precaution we should make the cake."

We all agreed. The flavor was optional, so we went with a vanilla cake with strawberries. We all had a slice.

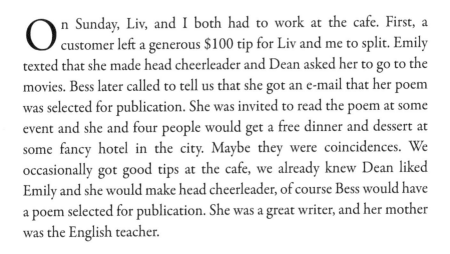

On Sunday, Liv, and I both had to work at the cafe. First, a customer left a generous $100 tip for Liv and me to split. Emily texted that she made head cheerleader and Dean asked her to go to the movies. Bess later called to tell us that she got an e-mail that her poem was selected for publication. She was invited to read the poem at some event and she and four people would get a free dinner and dessert at some fancy hotel in the city. Maybe they were coincidences. We occasionally got good tips at the cafe, we already knew Dean liked Emily and she would make head cheerleader, of course Bess would have a poem selected for publication. She was a great writer, and her mother was the English teacher.

But *maybe* the cake helped push the universe to make things happen a little faster. We couldn't wait to go to school on Monday and find out what other things would happen.

Chapter 25

MERANDA

It was nice having some time to myself *mostly* and to talk with Grandma a lot over the weekend. She made me what she called *Confidence Cookies* to arm me for a full week of school. I thought they helped because I woke up refreshed and ready to face the day on Monday morning.

The weekend brought Grandma and me closer. We went shopping in Boston together and we talked a lot in the car. I learned all about the different members of our family and heard stories from my grandma's youth. I accepted the fact that I was a witch and I had powers that I hadn't even discovered yet. Grandma told me about her coven. When she was my age, she had a group of friends, but they mostly drank tea and made beauty products. Her best friend was Grace's grandma Sofie.

Regretting how I acted toward Grace and the coven, I was happy when Mrs. Huddelson pulled up outside right as I was leaving for school. She waved me over to the car and offered me a ride, just as Grace came out of her house. Emily was sitting in the front seat and yelled for me to get in. Bess was sitting in the seat behind Mrs. Huddelson.

"Feeling better, I hope? I heard you were pretty sick," Mrs. Huddelson said, as I got into the seat behind Emily.

"Much better. Thank you. And thank you for the ride. I could have walked, but I appreciate it," I said, as Grace got into the car behind Mrs. Huddelson and Bess moved to the middle seat next to me, her arm brushing against mine. I glanced up at the rear-view mirror and Mrs. Huddelson was watching me. "I hope I didn't miss too much schoolwork."

Emily made a comment about how lucky we all were that there wasn't a lot of work in the first week of school because usually it gets piled on right away. Everyone was extra smiley and as we drove off to school, Mrs. Huddelson told me that Emily made head cheerleader. She talked so proudly about Emily, and it reminded me briefly of my mom and how she talked about me. The sadness tried to creep in, but I shrugged it away. I was determined to have a good day at school, a good week. I had a new outlook and I wanted to make the best of things.

"Aww Mom, it was nothing. Bess won a free dinner and dessert at a fancy hotel in the city and her poem was selected for publication. Now *that* is something to be proud of, "Emily said, smiling back at Bess whose face instantly turned bright red.

Everyone fussed over Bess and her accomplishments, and I could feel her heart racing. She was embarrassed, yet excited at the same time. I felt something else coming from her. It was like butterflies in my stomach, the way I felt when Leilani was around after we kissed, and our friendship changed. I couldn't tell if I was feeling this way toward Bess, or if Bess was feeling this way toward someone. I wasn't going to let the confusion distract me from the good day I was planning to have.

When we got out of the car Liv was just walking up. She had an early shift at the cafe and smelled like coffee. She gave me a puzzled look, then what seemed like a glare. Normally that would make me insecure, but Grandma's confidence cookies worked their magic on me. I didn't want to dwell on it. Emily and Liv rushed off and went into the school together. Bess and Grace walked slowly together as if waiting for me to catch up to them, after I finished profusely thanking Mrs. Huddelson for the ride. I offered to help her carry stuff into her classroom, but she declined.

When I caught up to Grace and Bess, I apologized for ghosting them. Then I whispered that I wanted to be part of their coven if they would have me.

"Oh, my Goddess, how lucky we are," Bess said excitedly.

"I don't think it's luck, but *fate*. No, *destiny*," Grace said.

At lunch, the five of us sat together at a table in the corner. We had the whole table to ourselves. Everyone talked quiet but excitedly about the spells we would learn and the power we would have combined. Liv seemed a little sarcastic when she talked, and I could sense some hostility coming from her. I assumed that was just her personality because nobody else caught on.

"So, what made you change your mind?" Liv asked me. I could sense fear in Bess and Grace who were sitting closest to me. If I could guess, I would say they were worried I would somehow change my mind if we discussed it.

"After I discovered one of my powers, I had to accept the fact that I am a witch and I really like hanging out with you guys," I said as everyone was suddenly extremely interested in what I had to say.

"What power did you discover?" Grace asked excitedly.

I scanned the area to make sure nobody else was listening. The girls noticed this and leaned in closer.

"I can breathe under water."

Liv gasped and stopped chewing her mouthful of carrot, then nearly choked as she inhaled and swallowed.

"You're lying," Liv said. This time I was certain she was glaring at me. "There's no way you can do that."

"Shut up and let her talk," Bess said, never taking her amazed eyes off me.

"I promise, I'm not lying. I had a flashback on Thursday on the way to school. I blacked out and lost time. I was just standing on the curb down the street. I had been walking to school and suddenly it was nine o clock." Everyone was hanging on my every word, even Liv.

"Then what?" Grace asked.

"During the flashback, I remembered the accident that killed my mom and brother. I was drowning, but when I let go and inhaled a bunch of water... I could breathe. That is how I survived," I said.

"That doesn't mean anything. You had a daydream. You are probably just trying to find an excuse to why your family died, and you survived," Liv snapped at me.

"Liv, what has gotten into you. That is uncalled for," Grace said as Bess and Emily seemed appalled.

"I'm sorry if you guys just want to think everything is sunshine and rainbows all the time and you want to bow down to the new girl, but I don't buy it. So, she had a daydream? That doesn't mean she can do it," Liv said.

Her words were venomous and stung for a second, but Grandma's Confidence Cookies continued to work, and I was sure of myself for the first time since I got to Holy Orchard.

"I'll prove it."

Chapter 26
GRACE

Standing at the edge of Holy Orchard High's Olympic size swimming pool, I wondered what insanity had brought us there. We could get in so much trouble sneaking into the pool after school hours. Liv got us in and planned what time would be best, since the swim team didn't practice on Mondays.

"You idiots better not get us caught. This could ruin my chance at getting team captain. I could probably even get kicked off the team," Liv said angrily, "Also, I'm going to be super pissed if I have to save your ass when you start drowning."

That was one of my fears, too. Not that we would get caught and Liv would get kicked off the swim team. I was worried that Meranda was wrong and could actually drown. I had faith though. She was our lost witch and if she drowned then our destiny would not come true.

We all wore our swimsuits so that if we did get caught, we could pretend we sneaked in to play in the pool, not that we were attempting to drown our friend. Meranda was wearing a navy blue and yellow one piece as she jumped off the diving board and dove gracefully into the water. The rest of us eased ourselves slowly into the water at the other end. Meranda swam over to us.

"Should we do it right here?" she asked.

"Yeah, I think it's safer that way. Then we are right here to help if anything goes wrong," I said.

"We need to figure out how we are going to do this. You might think I'm drowning and needing help, but I don't want anyone to try to *save* me... unless I'm unconscious and start floating," Meranda said.

"No way. By then it could be too late. How will we know?" Bess asked, her teeth chattering.

"Nothing's going to happen. We have luck on our side," Emily said.

"*We* ate the cake. *She* didn't," Bess said.

"Let's just do this and get out of here. I think we will know if she's drowning," Liv said, glancing up at the clock.

Meranda sucked in a deep breath, then lowered herself under the water. Suddenly she burst through the surface coughing and spitting out water, gasping for air.

"I told you. I *told* you. This was a complete waste of risking my chance at captain. I *knew* she couldn't do it!" Liv yelled angrily as she climbed up the ladder out of the water.

"No, wait! I can do it. I just have to figure out how. The first time, I was dying. My ability kicked in out of necessity. I needed to breathe to survive. It was different this time. I just don't understand how to control it," Meranda pleaded.

"Time's up. We need to get out of here before we get caught," Liv said ordering us out of the pool, waving her hands toward the locker room. Meranda looked so disappointed. Bess put her arm around Meranda and we all hurried into the locker room to get dressed.

Chapter 27

MERANDA

"If it makes you feel any better, at least you didn't drown," Bess said, her wet arm around my shoulders.

"I can do it. I *believe* I can do it," I said, not only trying to convince her, but also myself.

Maybe I was so sure of myself because of the Confidence Cookies my grandma made me. I shrugged the idea out of my mind. I could do it.

"Maybe there was too much pressure with everyone there?" Bess suggested, "Maybe we could try something smaller, like a bathtub. Just me and you? I could be there in case anything goes wrong. Maybe if you practice a little and figure out how to do it, then we could show everyone."

We didn't have time to dry off before leaving the school. The walk home was freezing, and the cold air was sharp against my skin as it blew toward us. A few blocks from school, we split up and went our separate ways, but Grace and I continued walking together. She tried to give me a pep talk. Despite the disappointment of not being able to convince them, I was still confident that I could do it.

I told Grace about Grandma's Confidence Cookies, but she reminded me that I could do it before I ate them. I had my flashback on Thursday and ate the cookies on Sunday.

We discussed the plan Bess had proposed and Grace said she believed it was a good idea. Maybe I had stage fright, or performance anxiety, whatever you want to call it. By time we reached our street, I felt better about the plan. I texted Bess to tell her we should try it.

O n Tuesday, Bess and I got permission to use the pool. I had been so focused on the task the day before that I hardly noticed Bess in her bathing suit, but that day I couldn't stop staring at her. She had on a black and turquoise one piece and there was just enough cleavage exposed to make me heart skip. I was feeling it again, the butterflies. I wasn't sure if I was feeling my own feelings, or hers.

We didn't even try to practice my breathing under water. There were other people around the whole hour. We spent most of the time swimming laps and we briefly joined a game of water polo before one of the teachers announced that free swim time was over. We needed to find somewhere else to go. The pool wasn't a reasonable option anymore. I wanted to avoid using a bathtub because they were too shallow, and it was too cold out to try a lake or ocean.

As we walked out of the locker room, I was stopped by the teacher who was watching our free swim time.

"You are the new girl from Hawaii," she said, "what's your name?"

"Meranda," I said, caught off guard, feeling like I was about to be scolded.

"Have you considered joining the swim team? I was watching you and you swim very well and you're fast. We need that."

I stared at her momentarily, having no idea what to say.

"Sorry, I'm Melanie Larson. I teach eleventh and twelfth grade P.E. and I coach the swim team."

There was a brief awkward silence while I weighed my options. Bess looked to me and shook her head "yes," encouraging me to answer.

"I was on the swim team back home. I wasn't planning to try out, but I guess I could," I said.

"You don't have to try out. Watching you today was all I needed. You're in. We meet Tuesdays, Thursdays, and Saturdays at 6:00 PM. There are also free swim times before and after school. Most of the team tries to make it a few times a week. Should I expect to see you at 6 tonight?"

I glanced at my watch. It was 4:15. Then I looked at Bess for an answer. She nodded.

"Yeah, I'll be here."

I called Grandma to pick us up and went home to get a bite to eat. Bess came with us, then Grandma dropped her off at home on the way back to school.

Liv was walking toward the school when I got dropped off. She seemed surprised and speed walked toward me. I could feel her heart rate increase and I could sense her anger.

"Why are you here?" she asked, trying to feign interest, and using a fake nice tone.

"I joined the swim team today," I said.

Liv's hands tightened into fists at her side and if looks could kill, I'd be dead. Suddenly her expression changed, and she smiled at me.

"Oh, that's wonderful. It would be a joy to be your captain," she said, then quickly sprinted toward the door.

When I got to the locker room, Mrs. Larson was there holding a clipboard and two swimsuits. She said she wasn't sure what size I was but guessed either a small or medium. I took the small and went to get changed. Thankfully, it fit, unlike my P.E. uniform.

We did a brief introduction, for my benefit since I was the only new person on the team. Liv spent most of the time glaring at me and fake smiling every time I noticed her. She even waved once. I couldn't understand why this girl hated me so much. What did I ever do to her?

We took turns doing timed laps, competing for the fastest times. Liv went first and I was last. She had the fastest time, and nobody could beat her, until I swam. My time beat hers by 3 seconds. Everyone cheered excitedly for me. Voices rang out, saying we would win for sure now that I was on the team. Liv wasn't around after that. She left in a hurry. She was dressed and out the door before I got into the locker room. The coach wanted to congratulate me and spent five minutes telling me how great our team was now that we had the two fastest swimmers in the region.

Liv spent the whole week being super nice to me, but I could sense it wasn't real. On Saturday, she was very smug. She couldn't wait to be announced swim team captain. Her happiness was cut short when Mrs. Larson announced that *I* was the new captain.

"This is a joke, right? There are cameras somewhere and I'm being *punked*," Liv said angrily.

"Actually, no. Meranda is the new team captain," Mrs. Larson said, "and you better choose your next words carefully because you are skating on thin ice right now."

"I don't understand. Did she even apply? She *just* started here. She doesn't even know anyone so how could she be a leader? She's not captain material."

"Liv, you are a great swimmer and an asset to this team, but you are not the captain. You haven't been very much of a team player or a leader lately. You get angry and are not supportive of your team. I'm sorry, but the team needs a leader who is willing to cheer them on and support them in defeat. I haven't seen much of that from you lately."

It was almost painful watching Liv beg for another chance and promise to do better. When Mrs. Larson told her it wasn't happening, Liv asked how she could possibly give me the captain position when nobody even knows me yet.

"What makes you think *she* is all of those things? You don't even know her!" she snapped, tears forming.

"I'll let this slide because you are upset, and I know how badly you wanted it. It was my decision and it's final. I don't have to explain myself, but I spoke with Meranda's previous coach about her abilities, and I am confident she will make a great team captain. Now I suggest you go get dressed and come back Tuesday with a better attitude. I won't accept insubordination, and neither will the team."

Liv stormed off and nearly slipped on a puddle of water. She regained her balance and slammed her palms against the door to the locker room, causing a loud thud to echo through the pool room. Mrs. Larson asked if I accepted the team captain position. I briefly considered as my new teammates cheered and yelled out words of encouragement. A girl named Mia nudged my shoulder and told me to say yes, so I did. I said I would be team captain. Part of me was excited, but the other part understood how angry Liv was. I wasn't sure if my friends would be angry or how this would affect the coven.

Chapter 28
GRACE

The buzz on social media was that the new girl from Hawaii made captain of the swim team and Liv was being nicknamed "Livid." Sometimes I really hated high school and the way teenagers could be so mean to each other all the time. I was excited for Meranda, but Liv wanted to be team captain so badly. I hated that she was being teased and mocked by everyone. I also worried that the tension between Liv and Meranda could have a negative impact on the progress we had been making as a coven. I wanted to nip this thing in the bud and called an emergency meeting of the coven. Unfortunately, Liv didn't show up.

Chapter 29
MERANDA

The next month went by amazingly fast. Everyone was busy with school, work, and extracurricular activities. Liv stayed on the swim team, but she didn't hang out with the team after practice, and she wouldn't talk to anyone in the coven. The rest of us spent our mutual free time trying to work on spells and learning to control our abilities. Even though I spent so much time in the pool, I didn't have time to practice breathing under water. Eventually, we stopped even mentioning it. I was sure that everyone thought I couldn't do it and maybe it was just a daydream after all. I was still positive I could and that I just needed to figure out how.

In mid-October, the idea of breathing under water nagged at me. I couldn't stop thinking about it, dreaming about it. I had a few more flashbacks but didn't lose any time. Bess was in the city with her parents and grandparents to have their free dinner and dessert at the fancy hotel and to read her published poem. We all got a copy of the publication, and I was proud that she was my friend.

The few times that Bess and I had gotten together to try my breathing under water, I spent most of the time feeling butterflies and not actually practicing the breathing. There were always people around and it never worked out for us to be truly alone. It was time to try it by myself.

All my friends were busy with their activities, Dad was at work and Grandma was out with a friend. I wore my swimsuit just in case I was wrong and happened to drown, so that I could save my dad and grandma the trauma of finding me dead *and* naked. I filled my grandma's claw footed tub with warm water and got in. I took a deep breath and laid down. With my eyes closed, I continued to hold my breath for as long as I could until the pain in my chest was unbearable.

Memories of the accident floated into my mind. I continued to hold my breath, fighting the pain, my head pounded angrily as if it would explode. Until I couldn't hold it any longer and I released, then sucked in, filling my lungs with water. My body writhed and I tried to sit up, but I couldn't. I was drowning.

Flailing my arms and legs, I panicked. I couldn't sit up. I couldn't breathe. I was dying. I could feel the water filling my lungs and swirling around inside. My chest and head hurt so bad, and I was extremely dizzy. Then suddenly, the water pushed out from slits in the sides of my neck. *Gills?* I instinctively took another breath through my mouth, sucking in water. My gills pushed the oxygen-removed water out and I could feel my heart beat slow as I calmed. My head stopped hurting and I felt clarity again. Was I a witch or a freaking mermaid? Either way, I could do it. I could breathe under water.

The next morning, I went to the free swim before school and only a few people were there. I pretended to hold my breath while I swam, but I remained calm and focused on my gills. Sucking water into my mouth, I used my gills to push it back out. I finally understood how to control it. It would be cheating to breathe under water to get faster swim times. I chose to hold my breath and not use my gills while competing. I was finally ready to show my friends what I could do.

The first person I told was Bess, when she got back from the city. Of course, I let her tell me all about how amazing the hotel was, the food she had and all the people she met first. It was nice to watch her talk excitedly about being a writer someday. I liked when she was happy, and I wasn't going to interrupt that. But later, I told her, and she was just as happy for me as I was for her. I could feel the butterflies and I was able to recognize the difference. Some of them were mine, and some were hers. We were both feeling it.

As we sat together, on the love seat in her living room, I leaned over and pressed my lips against hers. Something inside me ignited and our hearts raced in unison. She kissed me back slowly, for the longest five seconds of my life. Then my cell phone chimed that I had a text message.

Chapter 30
GRACE

Something was going on with Liv. Her anger and disappointment for not making swim team captain, and even losing out to Meranda, was understandable. But that was nobody's fault. We all tried to get Liv to hang out with us. She wouldn't even respond to anyone but Emily. Liv was the most interested in magic out of anyone I knew. Over the last month, she avoided us. She didn't come to coven meetings and had her grandmother schedule us on different shifts at the cafe. The coven was back to four members again and I could sense Emily pulling away. With Bess spending more time with Meranda, and Liv completely ditching us, Emily appeared to have lost interest in the coven as well.

Scrolling through social media on my phone, I stopped on a post from Holy Orchard High. It was a promotional flier for the HOH annual Halloween dance/party. Halloween was flying up fast. We hadn't even discussed costumes, or activities. I tapped the "share" button and tagged Meranda, Bess, Emily, and Liv.

"What should we wear?" I typed and hit *send*. Immediately, the familiar *...a friend is typing*, appeared on the screen.

Bess: oOoOoOoOo... not sure. Are we doing a group costume?

Me: That is what I was wondering. We could do something fun or scary.

Bess: or sexy. Ha-ha.

Meranda: I'm up for anything. Not sexy though.

Emily: I think Liv and I are going to pass.

Me: No way! Why?

Emily: Not feeling it.

Liv has untagged herself from your post.

Bess: Wow. Okay?

It was as though my heart was breaking. Liv and Emily were two of my best friends. I didn't want to blame Meranda, but she was kind of in the middle of our coven being torn apart. Liv was being ridiculous, but maybe Meranda shouldn't have accepted the team captain position. This was ruining everything. I put my phone down next to me and laid back on my bed, trying desperately to think of some way to fix it all. I believed whole-heartedly that we were meant to be a coven and friends forever.

I closed my eyes, inhaling deeply and releasing slowly to calm myself. Tinkerbell jumped up onto my bed, now big enough to have free reign of the house. She curled up in my neck and purred loudly. *Perfect timing, Tink.* Listening to the steady purring, I searched my mind for a solution. *Please Goddess, help bring our coven back together.*

"DEAN."

"What?" I gasped. As I sat up, I startled Tinkerbell from her sleep. I didn't recognize the voice, but someone clearly said, "Dean." I searched around the room and leaned over to look out my bedroom window. There was nobody there. "Hello? Mother?!" Nothing. Shaking my head, slightly disoriented, I got up and examined myself in the mirror of my vanity. "Dean!"

The realization hit me. Emily had been crushing on Dean for as long as I could remember. He asked her out, but they were both so shy about it that nothing had happened. If Dean went with us, we would at least be able to get Emily to come. If Emily came, maybe Liv would come, too.

Chapter 31
MERANDA

Time flew by as I floated through the week, and we were nearing the middle of October. Bess and I had been spending nearly every free moment together. We were even practicing magic outside of the coven. Over the weekend, Grace had to work at the cafe and Emily was cheering at the homecoming game. Bess and I agreed to skip the game and try some magic. Bess had taken cell phone pics of a few pages she liked in Grace's book. We flipped through the pictures, and one caught our attention. "Finding Your Spirit Animal/Recognizing Your Familiar."

Grace hadn't seemed extremely interested in that one, since animals were already attracted to her. Tinkerbell was most likely her familiar and she said she believed that a witch has many familiars during their lifetime. They come and go as we need them. We asked why her grandma had a spell in the book if they come and go on their own. She told us that some witches don't know how to recognize a familiar, even if it is staring them in the face. And some new familiars may need a gentle push to get started in their work.

The ritual was easy and only needed a single witch to make it successful, but Bess and I did it together. We simply needed to drink some tea, close our eyes and focus. We were to imagine ourselves on a journey alone, walking through a forest, or along a beach. When we find some sort of entrance or opening, we go inside and pay attention to what we see. At some point, we reach a fork and need to decide whether to go left or right. Eventually, we see light and emerge at the other end. We walk out of the forest or back onto the beach and will be greeted by our spirit animal. Once we know our spirit animals, we will be able to recognize our familiars when they come to us.

Grace had told us that she didn't plan to try the ritual. She didn't want to be tied down to one animal type. My grandma had told Bess and I that her spirit animal was a bumble bee and she had met thousands of them over her lifetime that helped guide her.

When Bess and I did the ritual, I imagined I was walking along the beach back home in Hawaii. Bess imagined walking through the forest. We didn't discuss the details of our imagined journeys because we didn't want to jinx it, but we couldn't keep our spirit animals a secret.

At the end of Bess's journey, she was greeted by a large crow. Of course, she would get a bird, she was air. Mine was confusing and I thought I had done my journey wrong.

Walking along the beach in Hawaii, I took notice of everything around me. The sand, the waves, the banana, and avocado trees. I came to an opening created by an entanglement of tropical plants, and I crawled through. I was walking in a rain forest and there was a path with a waterfall on one side and lush green plants on the other.

Continuing down the path, I came to a fork that went left and right. I stopped for a moment and considered both paths. The left went around the back of a wall of rocks behind where the waterfall was pouring down from. It was dark and I couldn't see extremely far without continuing down that path.

The right was lit up and I could see the path continue, plants on both sides and sun breaking through the large leaves. Something about the darkness of the left side called to me. The right was too obvious, so I went left.

I followed the dark path as vines and leaves crossed the ground in front of me, threatening to trip me, until finally there was light. When I emerged, I was on the beach again, waves crashing, the smell of salt in the air. And I was greeted by a beautiful fuzzy creature that stomped over to me with its fluffy tail in the air. A SKUNK.

I was sure I did the ritual wrong. I chose the wrong path. There were no skunks in Hawaii. Not native, not even brought over as pets. They were illegal. You couldn't even smuggle them in, so I should have chosen the obvious path. Of course, the path of darkness was meant to deter me, so I would choose the path of light. My spirit animal was probably swimming in the ocean. A dolphin or sea turtle. Maybe a shark. I was so angry at myself for messing up the journey and choosing the wrong path.

Bess giggled and kissed me.

"How would I get a skunk? Maybe I should try it again," I said, closing my eyes.

"Nah, I don't think you can do it wrong. Your spirit animal is a skunk," Bess said, plugging her nose and sticking her tongue out to tease me.

"It's not funny. I'm sad I did it wrong. I should have gotten a sea animal. Maybe a humuhumunukunukuapua'a."

"A humma what?" Bess asked, raising her eyebrows.

"A humuhumunukunukuapua'a. It means *triggerfish with a snout like a pig.* It's the state fish of Hawaii and is yellow and black and white. It has a pig nose and makes pig noises," I said, taking out my phone to show her a picture.

"Cool, but okay, in all seriousness. I really don't think you did it wrong. Skunks are beautiful and misunderstood, like you," she said in a flirting tone, "But, I mean, if you want to try it again, go for it."

I chose to not try again at that moment and opted to wait until later that night when I was alone. Instead, Bess and I watched a movie together. But when I was alone that night I repeated the journey, choosing the other path.

I came to the same fork in my path. I stopped and considered both directions. Again, left was dark and continued around the back of the rocks with the waterfall. And the right was all lit up with sun shining through the leaves. I was drawn to the left again, but I shook my head reminding myself I chose wrong before.

This time, I went right. The path was long and appeared to go on forever, but the plants and trees eventually parted, and the path came out onto the beach. I walked down to the water as I sensed something pulling me toward the ocean.

I walked quickly toward it, ready to meet my spirit animal, when something emerged from the tide. Wet fur broke the surface, as the animal waddled its way out of the water and shook out its coat before stomping over to me. It was a very wet SKUNK!

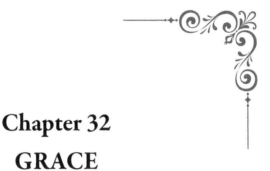

Chapter 32
GRACE

Dean agreed to go with us to the Halloween dance/party. He suggested we dress as superheroes, but I wanted to think it over and find out what the girls wanted to do. Of course, after finding out Dean was going, Emily changed her mind and decided she would go. Everything was coming together, and I just needed to find a way to get Liv to go, too. I traded shifts with Robin at the cafe so that I could work with Liv. My plan was to make it impossible for her to ignore me.

Liv glanced up as the bells on the door chimed to alert her of my entrance. Her eyebrows raised and she exhaled suddenly. Her surprised look turned into a glare as she lowered her eyebrows and stared at me.

"Hey Liv, it's nice to see you!" I said, putting my hands on her shoulders and hugging her from behind. Her tightened muscles relaxed, and she seemed to soften before my eyes.

"Hi... the table in the corner ordered four milkshakes. Can you get them?" Liv asked.

"Sure," I said. We were finally getting somewhere. We got a dinner rush soon after and didn't have a chance to talk, but I got my opening when we were clocking out.

"I really miss you. Like... a LOT. Please, will you come to the Halloween dance with us? Dean is even coming," I stared at her with pleading eyes. She could ignore my texts and avoid me on social media, but she couldn't say no to me in person, "Please! We always go."

"Not this year," she hesitated, "everyone is calling me 'Livid', and you are still friends with *Meranda*!"

"Is that why you don't want to go?" I asked, hugging her, "Liv, nobody is saying that anymore and Meranda didn't do anything wrong. We all just want to be friends again. We love you. Please?"

"I don't think so," Liv said, pushing past me.

"Wait! Please? Will you at least carve pumpkins with me?" my eyes stung as tears pushed their way to the surface. She wouldn't be able to resist my tears, but they were real, and it worked.

"Fine. When?"

I was happy. She still had a soft spot for carving pumpkins. It was our tradition. Every year we spent hours, over several days, carvings them, enough to line up on both sides to create a path from the street to my doorway. We did this so that my ancestors and lost loved ones could find their way to me to visit when the veil was thin on Halloween night. Liv never cared about doing it at her house because the only people she loved were still alive and she didn't care much about her ancestry. But this year was extra important. My father and grandmother were both gone now.

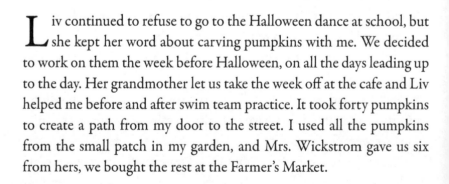

Liv continued to refuse to go to the Halloween dance at school, but she kept her word about carving pumpkins with me. We decided to work on them the week before Halloween, on all the days leading up to the day. Her grandmother let us take the week off at the cafe and Liv helped me before and after swim team practice. It took forty pumpkins to create a path from my door to the street. I used all the pumpkins from the small patch in my garden, and Mrs. Wickstrom gave us six from hers, we bought the rest at the Farmer's Market.

We spent the time watching Halloween themed and scary movies, while snacking on roasted pumpkin seeds and pizza. Both of our hands were red and sore from all the carving we had been doing. It was great. I had missed Liv so much.

We ended up with pumpkins carved with all kinds of faces. There were happy ones and scary ones. Liv even carved a few to resemble cartoon characters. We started out doing super detailed and intricate designs, to getting so tired we did the last half with traditional triangle shaped eyes and noses with zig zag mouths.

Sometime around carving the last few pumpkins, I asked Liv if she had been practicing magic at all.

"A little," she said, looking up at me. "A few spells here and there. Nothing major."

"Yeah, us too. A few things here and there. We should try to get the coven together and do something bigger."

"Oh?" she said, raising one eyebrow. "What do you have in mind?"

"We need to strengthen our individual abilities, and come together to do something big," I said, hoping she would have an idea that I could agree to, because I had nothing.

She sat up straight and stared at me with anticipation. She had all her attention on me, waiting for what my plan was. I took a deep breath, trying to desperately think of something to say.

"What's something you always wanted to try?" I asked, attempting to lead her to think of something.

"Uh, fly, breathe under water, create a love potion, bring back the dead, conjure money, know the answers to every question on every test, win all the time at everything, make things move with my mind, astral projection..."

"Woah, okay..." I said, stopping her. She would have gone on forever. "So, I didn't have anything specific in mind. But we do need to focus on our own abilities and strengths. Meranda can breathe under water, and your element is water so my guess is that you can probably do it, too. Maybe Meranda can teach you?" I suggested. She seemed to consider it for a second, then I sensed her anger.

"Not a chance."

"Why not? What is your problem with her?" I asked.

"I don't like her. I don't trust her. And I was here first, but now she shows up and takes over everything. My friends, my team, my captain position, breathing under water even. I tried that for months, probably even a year. I wanted it so bad, and she shows up and tries it a few times and *bam* she breathes under water," she said, balling up her fist and slamming it onto her thigh. Trying to be the peacekeeper again, I used my voice of reason.

"I really think that you and Meranda could be great friends and we all could come together and be super strong as a coven. Meranda didn't ask for any of this. Maybe you *can* breathe under water, and you will get there eventually. Maybe you can't, but there might be something else amazing that you can do. Distancing yourself from us isn't going to help. We need to do this together. We need to support each other."

Liv said nothing at first. She picked up one of the pumpkin carving tools and stabbed the pumpkin she was working on. I looked at her sternly waiting for her to say something.

"Please? Pretty please with a cherry on top," I shook my head at her, raising my eyebrows, "with whipped cream and sprinkles?"

"You know I don't like sprinkles," she said, a smile spread across her face.

"Fine. Anything you want. Name it. All I am asking is give it a chance. Give *her* and us a chance. Give us until the end of the year and if you want to bounce then fine. I will accept it and leave you alone about it. We can go back to being just the four of us."

"Okay. I'm in."

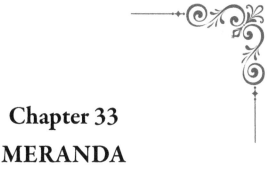

Chapter 33

MERANDA

The day before Halloween, Grace called a meeting of the coven. When Bess and I arrived, we admired the path of Jack-o-lanterns bordering the sidewalk that led to Grace's front door. Over the last couple of days prior, we watched the lines of pumpkins growing longer and longer. We were impressed by the amount of work that had gone into carving those pumpkins. Bess and I had each carved one pumpkin of our own and that was enough for me.

When we got up to Grace's bedroom, everyone was already there. Even Liv. Grace made a speech about teamwork and being there to support one another. Something about destiny and eternal friendship. It was hard to listen when I could sense Bess's heartbeat as she sat next to me. Grace cleared her throat loudly and everyone was staring at me.

"Sorry, I'm listening," I said, a little flustered. Bess smiled at me like she knew because she was counting the same butterflies in her stomach as I was counting in mine.

"I think we need to work on our individual powers. I did some research and found some powers that each element might possess. We might not have all of them, but we should try anyway," Grace said as she handed neon colored index cards to each of us. When she got to me, she gave me five cards.

I gave her a puzzled look after I realized they were labeled *Water, Fire, Earth, Air, Spirit.* Everyone else had only one card.

"I'm not sure yet what you are. My research was conflicting. I think you have water element abilities. But we already have a water element. You could be spirit, but you could also be a fifth element that some witches have discussed that have an affinity to water, fire, earth, and air. We don't know what you can do, yet. So, I think you should help Liv try to breathe under water and try some of the water spells, but you should also find out if you have any of the abilities held by the other elements."

I wasn't sure how to react. I could sense Liv's heart rate go up. She was angry but didn't show it on the outside. She smiled.

"When are we going to do this? How?" Emily asked, holding up her pink card.

"It's going to have to be next week. We have the Halloween party tomorrow, *Samhain* on the first, then Liv's birthday on the second."

I gasped out loud.

"The second is *my* birthday, too," I said. Liv, who was smiling seconds earlier, was suddenly unable to hide her irritation.

"Ugh, seriously?" she looked to Grace, "I told you. Every. Single. Thing. In my life."

Grace tried to redirect her immediately. Ignoring the tension in the room, Grace jumped up excitedly from her sitting position.

"This is great! We can go to Boston and make a day out of it. We can celebrate both of you in one day! Then we can work on our individual powers. Next weekend we will come together as a group and share our progress," Grace was beaming.

The final thing on the agenda for the coven meeting was a lecture on being more organized. Grace made us all download a calendar app on our phones and sync them, so that we know when we have free time to meet. She didn't let us leave until Liv and I agreed on a date and time to work on our powers together. We would rip the bandage off and start on the third, the day after our joint birthday celebration.

Chapter 34
GRACE

Certain that Meranda and Liv could be great friends if they only tried, I was hopeful. Things were finally right again. Everyone agreed to go to the Halloween party, even Liv. We didn't have enough time to plan a group costume, and no one liked Dean's idea of doing a superhero theme, so we wore whatever we wanted.

I selected my green witch's hat that I had adorned with fake leaves, and I paired it with a green floral dress and combat boots. Liv dressed as a vampire, wearing all black and fake pointy teeth. We planned to meet everyone else at the party, unsure of what to expect.

When we arrived at the school, the gym was transformed since we had seen it only mere hours earlier. There were inflatable ghosts and pumpkins, a skeleton pirate ship, and webs of spiders everywhere. In the corner, where the bleachers normally sat, was a scene of witches standing around a cauldron. There was a photo op area that had cardboard cutouts of a witch, a pirate, and a ghost that people were already taking cell phone pics of their friends in.

Liv and I found our way to the concession stand which was being run by Mr. Ritter and Emily's mother. The PTO (Parent Teacher Organization) made caramel and candy apples that were for sale. There were popcorn balls, hot apple cider, and pizza slices. Liv and I each bought a hot apple cider and made our way through the growing crowd of costumed students. A DJ was at the other end playing a mix of Halloween party themed music and current dance hits.

We recognized Emily and Dean immediately when they walked in. Dean was dressed as a muscular Superman and Emily was Wonder Woman. It was a little suspicious for last minute costumes, especially since Dean wanted to dress as superheroes two weeks earlier. I made no comment on this because Emily and Dean seemed so happy. I was really rooting for them.

We stood in a group talking together with some of the football players and cheerleaders for a while. Finally, Bess and Meranda walked in. Bess was dressed as Little Red Riding Hood and Meranda was wearing a pirate costume. Everyone looked great. We all spent the night dancing, eating, and laughing. It was like old times again. The night passed in slow motion as I watched the smiles and laughter across my friends' faces. Everything was going to work out.

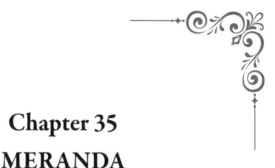

Chapter 35
MERANDA

The Halloween Party at school was fun. Bess and I went for a walk alone before we were expected to meet up to go back to Grace's for a sleepover. There were dead leaves and apples all over the ground. I was getting used to the cooler East Coast air, but the short sleeves of my tunic left my arms bare. Goosebumps crept up from my wrists to my shoulders. Bess turned to face me and put her hands on my upper arms.

"You are so cold," she said, trying to warm me up by rubbing her palms against my skin.

"Yeah, it happens," I said, trying to be cool while I was freezing my butt off.

"I'll share my warmth with you," Bess said in a flirting tone, as she moved closer to me and draped her red hooded cloak around us.

The butterflies were too much, and I leaned forward to kiss her. As my lips pressed against hers, I floated. The leaves rustled and the air grew warmer. I opened my eyes and gasped as the fallen leaves whirled around us.

"Are you doing that? How?" I asked.

"Oh that?" Bess said nodding at the leaves, "that's nothing. I've been swirling leaves for as long as I can remember."

"Are you making the air warmer? Is that you?" I asked, impressed. She nodded.

"I've been practicing. I've noticed my magic is stronger when I am touching another witch. Kiss me," she said, licking her cherry-stained lips. So, I did.

The leaves rustled and the warm air circulated around me, then there was a pressure I couldn't explain. I opened my eyes just in time to see all the fallen apples floating in the air, then fall to the ground as I pulled my lips away from Bess.

"Wow, is that new?" I asked, hugging her tighter.

"That's the first time I did it that long. I've been trying for heavier objects, but they never stay up," she said, and I could feel her heart beating faster.

Finally, I was able to tell the difference between emotions, based on how the heart was beating. She was incredibly happy and so was I. Our hearts were beating in unison. We were about to kiss again, when Emily and Dean walked up from the side of the school. They stopped and kissed.

"Wooo, go girl!" Bess said excitedly, loud enough that only I could hear, "guess we aren't the only ones feeling the love tonight." She tensed up and I could briefly feel her fear. "Well, not love, but you understand what I mean," she giggled.

I was suddenly insecure, unsure if she just accidentally mentioned love because she loved me, or she backtracked because she didn't. There was a strange air of awkwardness between us as Bess suggested we run and catch up with Emily and Dean.

Emily's mom gave us all a ride in her minivan, even Dean. She dropped Dean off first, then brought the rest of us to Grace's house for a sleepover. The night had started out magical, but toward the end I had this awful sense of impending doom. I thought of Leilani and where we were in our relationship when everything went to Hell. She was my best friend, and it took years to get where Bess and I were, after only a few weeks. It was much slower with Leilani, but we were at almost the same place that Bess and I were.

Leilani and I said we loved each other all the time. We said it before romantic feelings were ever realized. But the first time we said it for real, was the night before the accident. Part of me felt like I was being punished for being happy. How could I forget my mom and Rocco so easily, just because a cute girl was interested in me?

Chapter 36
GRACE

My mother promised to stay upstairs and give us privacy for our sleepover, and she kept her word. We pulled the cushions off my oversized sectional in the living room to make a giant bed on the floor. We spent the first part of the night discussing the most important moments of the party. The costume contest that none of us were even nominated for. We decided next year we would plan something amazing ahead of time. The awesome pics we all took and spent a half an hour posting on social media. Then there was the unavoidable coupling that happened.

Emily was so happy. We all got to witness Dean give her a quick kiss goodbye as he got out of the minivan and her mother sang "Emily and Dean sitting in a tree." Her cheeks were still pink from all the blushing she was doing on the way to my house. She had been crushing on Dean for years and it was official now that they were a couple.

"I'm not the only one. Meranda and Bess were practically making out by the apple trees," Emily said, turning all the attention off herself. Meranda and Bess stared at each other, their faces turning red. They both looked down at the same time and I could tell something was going on. It was weird, so I changed the subject to give them a way out.

"So, has anyone tried any of the powers on the cards I gave you?" I asked.

"I can warm the air around me and float apples for a short time, if I am touching another witch. I was also able to eavesdrop on a conversation from two blocks away. Nothing interesting to report, though," Bess said.

"That's great. That is a huge start. Anyone else?" I asked, looking around at Meranda, Liv and Emily.

"I'm still working on my fire powers. I can light a candle with little effort and put out a campfire easily. I can *start* a small campfire, but it is difficult and takes a lot out of me. I want to get to the point that I can start big fires easily and put them out. I also don't think I can touch fire without being burned. I burned my hand baking cookies and it hurt when I put my hand too close to the flame on my candle," Emily said.

"Well, maybe it's something you can learn to do. Maybe it will happen as you get stronger. Or maybe you won't, so don't try to get too close to any big fires. But this is great," I said, looking to Liv then Meranda, "what about you?"

Meranda took a deep breath and seemed to consider her words.

"I can breathe under water as we all know. I can manipulate and overpower other people's emotions, but I have no control over when that happens. I can also feel heartbeats and what other people are feeling. I've also been having lucid dreams where I feel like I am really there. I don't know if that is anything," Meranda said, then opened her mouth like she was going to say something else, but then she didn't.

"Meranda and I did a ritual to find out what our spirit animals are," Bess said. I was surprised and felt a little violated because that would mean they used a spell from my grandmother's book without asking me. But I was also happy that they were doing magic.

"And?" I asked, waiting for the results.

"I got a crow. I haven't been approached by my familiar yet, but I have seen a lot of crows everywhere I go now. It's as if they are following me," Bess said, smiling.

I briefly reconsidered my initial feelings of not wanting to do the ritual for myself. I was worried I would get a certain animal and be tied to one species. What if it was a dog? Would that mean Tinkerbell was just a plain animal off the streets with no magical connection to me whatsoever? I was torn, but extremely interested in the ritual. Bess and Meranda told me about their journeys and how it felt. The tea was also bitter because it was chamomile and lavender with dandelion root, no sugar allowed. I was curious what animal I would get and made a mental note to try it later. Meranda was hesitant to tell us the results of her journey, but I asked her anyway.

"A skunk," she said, grunting afterward. Everyone was surprised and talked all at once.

"A skunk? That would probably be an animal I would get. Have you noticed any around?" I asked.

"No, never. I even repeated the ritual and tried to focus on the ocean, sure I would get a sea animal and a skunk came out of the water. I have never seen a skunk in real life, and I think I did something wrong."

"No, I don't think you can mess it up. The universe shows you what you are supposed to see. If you were shown a skunk, twice even, then your spirit animal is a skunk. You should probably keep an eye out for them. I'm sure they are around. This is great," I said.

After finding out Meranda got a skunk, I was even more curious about what animal I would get. A skunk. That is not typical for a water element. I was sure she was a 5th element. I turned to Liv.

"What about you?"

"I've been trying to freeze water. I'm getting there. So far it turns a little slushy. I've also been working on pulling water from the air. And," she hesitated. "Meranda is going to work with me to try to find out if I can breathe under water," she said in a voice that seemed like she was trying to be nice. I could tell she wanted to lash out or say something mean, but I was proud of her for trying to get along.

Things were falling together nicely. The Halloween dance went very well. Everyone was getting along and working on their powers. I couldn't wait until we were strong enough. I believed whole heartedly that once we were stronger, we would be able to come together and summon my grandmother's spirit. I wanted to see her and talk to her again, at least one more time.

Chapter 37
MERANDA

The day after Halloween, we had a *Samhain* celebration at my house, organized by my grandma. Grandma invited my aunts, my cousin Dean, Grace and her mom, Bess, Emily, and Liv. Dad went golfing after explaining to me that he didn't believe in all this *mumbo jumbo*. I wasn't so sure about it, but my friends were really into it.

Grandma had baked a bunch of "soul cakes" which she explained were for our ancestors and we were going to have a *dumb supper*. This was often done on October 31st, but it was tradition in our families to do this on November 1st. I had no idea what a dumb supper was or what soul cakes were, but Grace and my grandma were happy to fill me in.

We sat in Grandma's formal dining room at the long table before any other guests arrived. It was just me, Grandma, and my friends. I was already familiar with sugar skulls and marigolds because my *Kapuna* had Mexican roots. But this was different from what I expected for Day of the Dead.

"Witches in the Northern Hemisphere celebrate Samhain on November first. Some celebrations begin on Halloween. It has been a tradition of mine and Grace's grandmother's that we have passed down to our children and grandchildren to have a Dumb Supper on Samhain or November first," Grandma started. "What's a dumb supper you may be wondering?"

I nodded.

"We bake *soul cakes* which are filled with our intentions, and we serve them with dinner to our dearly departed loved ones," Grandma continued, before she was interrupted by Liv.

"The person who gets the burnt one gets to be the human sacrifice," Liv snarled.

"Oh Dear, you are funny," Grandma said, lowering her eyebrows at Liv, "yes, this happened in pagan traditions, but definitely does not happen now. We are smarter than that. We do not do any type of human or animal sacrifices like our ancestors used to do."

"Ok, I still don't understand what a dumb supper is," I said, confused.

"It's a dinner honoring our loved ones who had passed away, and we invite them to sit at the head of the table. The catch is that the dinner is completely silent," Grandma said. I raised my eyebrows at her communicating that this was a stupid idea.

"It's incredibly beautiful. The veil is thin at Samhain and allows spirits to visit us. Anyone who passed away this year and may have been unable to crossover to the other side is finally able to do that at Samhain," Grace said, convincingly.

"I'm not sure I believe that," I said.

"You can breathe under water and control people's emotions, but you're not sure you believe that?" Liv asked, rolling her eyes at me. I wasn't sure what I felt. Was I supposed to believe that my mom and Rocco would be able to come for dinner? How boring would it be to sit in silence eating dinner?

"We light candles at the head of the table for each of our loved ones," Grandma started again, "Before the dinner, we write a note with what we would like to say to them. We will shroud the spirit chair in a cloth that my mother gave to me on my wedding day. We will smudge the room to keep away any negative energy, then we will light the candles and form a circle inviting our deceased loved ones, thus setting our intentions. I, as the host, will be seated at the other end of the table and I will serve everyone. Once everyone is served, we eat in silence."

"Won't that be hard for my little cousins?" I asked, genuinely concerned.

"Dean will be here, but the other boys are not that far along in their spiritual journeys yet. They have other plans for the evening," Grandma said. Emily blushed at the mention of my cousin's name.

"So, we eat in silence, then how do we know when we can talk again?" I asked.

"We eat in silence and wait for everyone to finish. This requires patience. Once we are finished, we set our utensils down, place our hands in our laps and wait," Grandma put her hands in her lap as she explained.

"Then what? Grandma, the suspense is killing me," I said, because I was getting annoyed that she was taking forever to tell me everything.

"Then we take turns walking up to the head of the table and find the candle for each of our departed loved ones and burn the note in their flame. When everyone is finished, we say a silent prayer for the spirits, then we take turns standing up and leaving the room in silence. On your way out, stop at the spirit chair, say goodbye silently to your loved ones. We leave the candles burning overnight and, in the morning, they should be out on their own, signifying that the spirits have crossed back over to the other side, until we meet again next year." Grandma finished.

Everyone stared at me, waiting for my response. I was interested in the possibility of leaving a note for my mom and Rocco. There were so many things I wanted to say to them. The tears welled up behind my eyes at the thought of it. I choked back the tears and inhaled deeply.

"Okay. I'm in," I said, softly. Then I went upstairs to write my notes privately, as the girls helped my grandma cook and set the table.

I sat down at the hand carved wooden desk in my bedroom, pulled a notebook from the drawer and put my pen to the paper on the first page.

Dear Mom,

It was strange to write "Dear Mom." In all the times we had written each other notes, we never wrote "Dear." We would never be that formal. I tore the page out of the notebook, crumbling the paper and tossing it in the wastepaper basket next to my desk. I started again.

Mom,

Guess what?! I'm a witch. And I survived the accident because I can breathe under water.

No. That was wrong. I tore the page out and threw the crumpled ball into the trash. It was so strange to write a note to my dead mom. It was hard to think of what to say and the tears came uncontrollably. I started at least five more notes and ended up crumbling them all into balls. Finally, I knew what I wanted to say.

Mom,

I miss you. Words cannot describe the ache I have in my heart from losing you and Rocco. I miss our sailing and hiking adventures. I am not sure what I believe anymore because my life surprises me every day. My only hope is that you and Rocco are safe and happy together, wherever you are. May you have a safe journey to the other side, and I look forward to our visit next year. I love you, Mama.

Love Meranda

It was short and to the point. It felt right. I honestly could have written a twenty-page letter easily, if I had said everything I wanted to say, but this felt right. Then it was time to write Rocco's letter. I was already crying from writing Mom's but thinking of Rocco made me completely bawl my eyes out. Rocco was hard. I couldn't even put pen to paper until I had the letter written perfectly in my mind.

Rocco,

My sweet baby brother, I miss you terribly. There were so many things I wanted to show you and it breaks my heart thinking of all the things that could have been. You were so tiny, and I was proud to be your big sister, from the moment you were born. I promise to always strive to be the big sister you looked up to, to be worthy of the title. I love you with every ounce of my being. Promise me, you will always stick by Mom. I will visit with you next year.

Love Mana

The tears were flowing heavily, and snot was pouring from my nose. It was so unfair. We had the same genes. We both had witch's blood. Why did I survive and not him? Why did I have the powers, but he didn't? He was so young. I wiped my tears on my sleeve and grabbed a tissue to blow my nose, then there was a knock on my bedroom door.

Chapter 38
GRACE

Meranda had been upstairs for over an hour. I thought it would be a good idea to check on her and see how her letters were coming along. I went upstairs and knocked on her bedroom door.

"Come in," she said.

As I walked in the door, she sat at her desk, wiping away tears with two folded pieces of paper in front of her.

"I came to check on you... find out if you needed any help with your letters," I said, sounding more like a question than a statement. Then I reached out to hug her, which she accepted.

"I was just thinking how unfair it is that Rocco died. He had witch's blood, too. Why did he have to die?" She said, hiccupping.

"Well, not every witch has powers, and he was so young. Dean is a witch, but he doesn't seem to have any powers. Some powers are passive. I'm sorry you lost him. It really isn't fair. I'm sure he was a beautiful soul with so much potential," I said, trying to comfort her with both my words and my arms. She softened as she hugged me back.

"Thank you. It's really hard," she said.

"I understand. I never lost a sibling, but I lost people. I was so close to my father when he died. And my grandmother was like my best friend. It really does get easier, like people say. You will think of them and no longer ache, tears no longer come. You can remember things about them and smile and even laugh. I feel like they are with me all the time, especially when the veil is thin at Samhain. It gives me comfort to realize that I can still communicate with them, even if I can't see them."

I said the words and they were mostly true. I didn't tell her that I sometimes wake up from dreams that are so real and cry because I thought my father or grandmother were still alive and had to lose them all over again. I almost told her, at that moment, of my plan to summon my grandmother's spirit once we are strong enough as a group. I almost gave her hope of doing the same with her mother and brother, but I thought better of it.

"Are you ready to come downstairs and check out the dining room? It looks ah-maazing!" I said, cheerfully as I nodded toward the door. "Also, Bess is downstairs looking like a little lost puppy without you, just saying."

Meranda laughed and we headed for the door, the smell of apple pie and stuffed squash wafting up the stairs and down the hallway to her room.

"I set your place at the table next to Bess," I said, winking at her.

Chapter 39

MERANDA

The dumb supper, although strange, was cool. Grandma had a black tablecloth, with mostly black cloth napkins. The plates were white and black and there were little vases of marigolds placed in the center of the table. The head of the table had a chair with a black and white cloth draped over it. There were black candles unlit at the end of the table. I counted ten. Grandma saw me studying them.

"There are ten. I think I have enough. One for my Samuel and one for Sarah. One each for your aunts' two husbands who passed away. One for Grace's dad and one for her grandma. One for Bess's grandma and one for Emily's grandma. One for your mom and Rocco. Am I missing anybody?" Grandma asked to the room.

"I don't think so," Grace said.

"Are you sure there isn't anyone in your life who has passed away?" Grandma asked. She was talking to Liv.

"Nope. Everyone who matters to me is still alive," Liv said, crossing her arms.

My aunts and Dean arrived, and we sat at the long dining room table. My grandma lit all ten candles, then we joined hands in silence. Without anyone speaking, everyone knew what to do and I just followed along. Grandma smudged the room by burning sage and fanning it slowly around every corner of the room. We set our intentions and said a silent prayer.

Grandma scooped food on everyone's plates, including one at the head of the table. There was stuffed acorn squash from Grandma's garden that had meat, rice, and veggies inside. Meatless for Grace. Grandma also served corn and mashed potatoes and a smaller plate with two soul cakes for each of us. Then she sat down and nodded her head. The dinner was silent, and everyone took it seriously. I expected immature snickers from someone, anyone. But nobody laughed. Nobody looked around or smiled. They just ate their food. I sensed love coming from all of them and it gave me butterflies.

I ate quickly because I didn't want to be the last one eating, holding everyone else up. My grandma and Grace were the last ones done, finishing about the same time. Then one by one, everyone got up and stood at the head of the table, finding the candle that represented their loved one and burning the letter that matched it.

When it was my turn, I walked over to the head of the table and found the two candles for my mom and Rocco. There was a leaf with a name printed on it next to each candle. I found the ones that said *Kalani* and *Rocco*. I held my mom's letter in my hand and considered everything I wanted to say to her then I put the corner into the flame of the candle. As the flame spread over the folded piece of paper, I placed it in the ash bowl, where everyone had set their burning letters. Then I found Rocco's candle and did the same.

It felt like my mom was with me. Her voice was even in my head. It was like she was telling me she was alright. I was at peace. I pictured Rocco and I playing in the sand and imagined that he was somewhere building a giant sandcastle.

Liv was the last person remaining and I thought her turn would be skipped, but she got up like everyone else and went to the head of the table. She closed her eyes and stood silently for a few moments, then she took a piece of paper out and lit the end with one of the candles. I didn't see which one. I was surprised and glanced around the room but nobody else seemed to notice. Liv placed the burning paper in the ash tray and sat back down. We said our silent prayer, then one by one we got up and gave our soundless goodbyes at the end of the table and filed out of the room. Grandma made sure the last letter was completely burned and that the candles were secure on the table, before leaving the room with the rest of us.

"That was intense," I said, whispering to Bess, "Who did Liv write a note for?"

"Huh? I didn't see anything. I was thinking of my grandma," she said with a questioning glare.

"She totally went up there and burned a note on one of the candles, but I didn't see which one," I said. "Which one do you think it was?"

"Maybe it was Grace's grandma. Liv and Grace were best friends for over a decade. She had to have gotten close to her grandma," Bess said. She was probably right, so I let it go.

I somehow felt better after saying goodbye to my mom and Rocco. Like I finally had some closure and knowing that they were okay. I wouldn't mind continuing this tradition with Grandma every year.

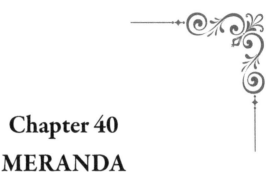

Chapter 40
MERANDA

When I woke up the next morning, I went into the dining room. All the candles were burned out except Rocco's. Weird. Grandma said it was probably because he was so young, his spirit was just so full of light and energy. That made sense. He had tons of energy.

Grandma was a little disappointed that I didn't want to have a big sweet sixteen party, but she made me some birthday cupcakes and a cup of tea for breakfast. Then I left with the girls for Boston. As much as I didn't want to, I brought a gift for Liv. It was her birthday, too, after all.

Her gym bag she used for swim practice was getting old. I figured she could have used a new one. I found one that looked like her old bag in a boutique downtown. When Liv opened the gift, she seemed happy. She told me she had been too busy with practice and working at the Cafe, but she would find something for me on our trip. She sounded genuine, but with my experiences I have had with her, I wasn't going to hold my breath.

We stopped at Vinny's Pizza for lunch. It was the same place my dad took me on our way to Holy Orchard from the airport.

When the waitress came to our table and gave us our menus, we ordered our drinks. Root beer in frosty mugs all around.

"Birthday girls' choice, my treat. Order anything you want," Grace said, proudly.

"I'll have a small ham and pineapple pizza," I said, not even considering the menu, "but you don't have to pay. Thank you, though."

"I insist. It's your birthday and it would make me incredibly happy to treat you," Grace said quite convincingly.

"We can share a vegan sausage and pineapple pizza, Grace. Thank you. I really appreciate it," Liv said, smiling happily. She was different to me. Either that or my original perception of her was all off.

"Oh, you don't have to order what I like. Please, get anything you want," Grace said.

"I assure you; I want the vegan sausage and pineapple pizza. Maybe your veganism is rubbing off on me," Liv said, winking at Grace.

"I would totally share a pizza with any of you, but I don't think pineapple belongs on pizza and vegan cheese tastes like feet," Emily said, "Bess, you want to share a pepperoni with extra cheese?"

Bess nodded, just in time for the waitress to bring us our drinks.

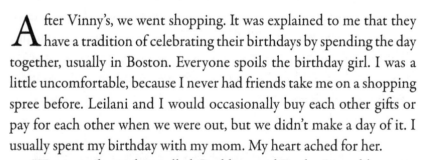

After Vinny's, we went shopping. It was explained to me that they have a tradition of celebrating their birthdays by spending the day together, usually in Boston. Everyone spoils the birthday girl. I was a little uncomfortable, because I never had friends take me on a shopping spree before. Leilani and I would occasionally buy each other gifts or pay for each other when we were out, but we didn't make a day of it. I usually spent my birthday with my mom. My heart ached for her.

We stopped at a place called Cauldron and Books. It was like a new age bookstore/cafe. Liv bought me a necklace with a Triple Goddess pendant. She smiled kindly when she gave it to me. I was afraid to let my guard down, but happy that we were making progress in our friendship.

By the end of the day, I had gotten the necklace from Liv, a deck of tarot cards from Emily, a gorgeous journal with a mermaid on it from Grace and a throw blanket and scarf from Bess. We visited a museum and stopped for ice cream. Then we headed home.

Emily was driving and had borrowed her mom's minivan. She dropped me and Grace off first. I walked up the sidewalk to my house and there was movement on the porch. I stopped and tried to see what it was, some sort of animal. I crept slowly toward the porch until I could get a closer glimpse. The motion light turned on, startling me and I saw it. The familiar black and white fur from my spirit animal journey. It was a skunk, and it was waiting for me.

Chapter 41
GRACE

After the amazing weekend I had with my friends, I woke up refreshed and ready for school. The day was uneventful, and everyone else was busy with extracurricular activities after school. My mother was working in her shop, and I had the house to myself. I tried again, for the umpteenth time, to summon my grandmother.

First, I burned sage and lavender to banish any negative energy from my space. I set my grandmother's spell book on my vanity and opened it to the page titled *Summon the Dead*. I briefly read over the words in the spell, not that I needed to because I had it memorized months ago.

Pulling the chalk from the wooden box on my vanity, I drew a circle on my bedroom floor, carrying the box with me. I pulled out five candles, one by one, setting them equal distance from each other on the circle, then lighting them with a match. The smell of sulfur wafted through my nostrils fighting the sage and lavender and slightly overpowering it.

I gently grasped from inside the box, the handle of my athame, a dagger made of glass with flowers permanently suspended inside. Setting the box on the floor near the circle, I turned the dagger over in the palm of my left hand and gently ran my fingers over the pentagram engraved on the handle. My first athame. My grandmother gave it to me as a gift for my thirteenth birthday. A friend of hers had made it just for me. My mother threw a fit that day, saying I was too young to have one, but my grandmother knew I was ready.

I smiled at the memory and held the athame in the air, calling for the spirit element. Facing the East, from inside the circle, I pointed my beloved dagger out and called for the element of air. I moved clockwise and called for each element, until I ended on North, my earth element. I was attuned to each element and sat in the middle of the circle. Then I pictured my grandmother, imagining her standing in front of me and said the words I had memorized.

"Hear my pleas, hear my cries, spirit from the other side, I beg of you, cross now and join me earth side," I said aloud. Nothing happened. I repeated the words, my voice cracking more each time. "Hear my pleas, hear my cries, spirit from the other side, I beg of you, cross now and join me earth side." Nothing. I repeated louder, until my tears were too much. "Grandmother, it's okay. We're getting stronger. I will see you soon."

I closed the circle by standing to face North, holding my athame out and slowly pulling it back to me.

"Earth, thank you. I release you," I turned counterclockwise and repeated for all the elements, then held my dagger into the air, "Spirit, thank you. I release you."

Wiping my tears on my sleeve, I kneeled to blow out the candles and used a wet wipe to clean the chalk from my floor. I was a little defeated, but I was still hopeful, knowing that the coven was back together. My friends were all getting along and practicing. Liv was opening up to working with Meranda. *Soon.* Soon we would be strong enough to summon her. I'd waited so long already; I could wait a little longer.

Chapter 42
MERANDA

Liv and I went straight to the pool after school to try breathing under water before the swim team came in for extra practice. We had a swim meet coming up on Friday and needed to practice our times. We weren't the only ones who came early, and it was difficult to give her any pointers with everyone there. Liv was clearly getting frustrated, and I sensed her anger and hostility toward me was increasing. The only thing that worked for me was almost drowning. There was no way we were going to get away with trying that with half the team in the pool with us, but we both made a promise to Grace.

"We can pretend like we are doing underwater breathing exercises. That's normal and totally not suspicious right?" I asked Liv, cupping my hand over my mouth as I moved closer to her.

"Yeah, pretend like you are timing me, *Captain*," she said in an overly fake-nice tone. I brushed it off and held up my wrist, tapping the stopwatch feature on my new waterproof fitness band. Dad surprised me with it a day late for my birthday. In his defense, I was gone most of the day on my actual birthday and I did love it.

"Ok, so just go under and hold your breath as long as you can. When you think you can't hold it any longer resist the urge to come up for air. If you can breathe under water, this will work," I whispered loudly into her ear, but there was so much noise in the pool that no one else could hear me.

"Got it, *Captain*," she said, in that tone again.

Liv took in a deep breath and was about to go under, as two guys from the team came hurdling toward us. One bumped Liv, in the shoulder knocking her into me and we both lost our footing and went under. That wasn't the first time that has happened and definitely wouldn't be the last. The boys liked to screw around in the pool when they should be practicing their times.

"Sorry, ladies. We are getting a game of water polo together; would you like to join us?" Mason Hartley said, batting his eyelashes at Liv, as a wet blond curl fell into his face. I could feel her heart beating faster and her mood shifted from annoyance to something positive. She was crushing on him. I could tell. I didn't think Liv liked anyone.

"Liv and I are participating in the swim meet on Friday, so we have a lot of practice to get in. Maybe next time," I said, hoping Liv wouldn't be terribly upset that I sent the boys away.

"Alright, your loss," Mason said, nodding for the other boy whose name I didn't know because he wasn't on the team, to go with him. Liv smiled in a way I never saw her smile before, as she watched them swim to the other side of the pool.

"Let's just forget it for now. Our focus should be on practicing for the swim meet. After that we should have time in the pool to ourselves," Liv said, and I agreed.

At the meet, I signed up for three events and Liv signed up for four. We were both in the relay. Liv had been getting consistently faster times than me, only by a second or two. I didn't mind. I just loved swimming and racing. I didn't have to always win.

In Liv's last event before the relay, she was doing great and we were all cheering her on, believing she would get the fastest time. She did and climbed out of the pool smiling. Her smile quickly faded as she was told she was disqualified.

"What? Are you kidding me?" she said defensively to the official.

"You failed to touch the wall with both hands when executing your turn," the official told her.

"What? I *did* use both hands," she said angrily.

The official put up her hands as if to say she wasn't going to argue and walked away. Liv was flustered and sitting with her arms crossed, waiting for the relay race that we both were signed up for.

Two of our teammates were up before us. They both kept a good time, and we were in the lead, then Liv was up next. She dove in, started out strong, then something happened. Liv suddenly went under water and struggled in her lane. Everyone stood, with concern on their faces, including me. It looked like she was caught in an invisible net. Someone was about to jump in after her, when suddenly she was released. She gasped for air momentarily then hurried to catch up. By time I got in, it was too late to recover the race. I swam as fast as I could, and we still got last place with the slowest time. When I climbed out of the pool, Liv got in my face.

"I know what you did. It was you!" she pointed her finger in my face.

"What? I didn't do anything," I said, confused as she stormed off to the locker room.

Chapter 43
GRACE

I had been emotional all week, but somehow hopeful, after my failed attempt at summoning my grandmother. I wasn't expecting to hear from Liv Friday night since the swim meet was out of town, so I was surprised when she called. She said she needed to talk to me ASAP and that she was getting a ride with a team mate instead of waiting for the bus, since she was done with all her events.

Liv got dropped off at my house 45 minutes later and I could tell she had been crying. Her face was all red and splotchy, and she kept sniffling.

"What happened?" I asked, reaching out to hug her. She fell into my arms, releasing the sobs she had been trying to hold in. "Talk to me, Liv!"

"Meranda is out to get me. You have to see that!" she shouted between sobs.

"Why do you think that?" I asked, pulling back, and staring her in the eyes.

"She sabotaged me today. I was disqualified from a race I won because I didn't touch with both hands, but I *did*. Then, in the relay, I was swimming," she hiccupped, "and I got pulled under and I felt like I was in a fishing net. We lost the race because I was sabotaged."

My heart drop to my stomach at Liv's accusation. I didn't believe Meranda would sabotage her, and I told her that.

"Wasn't Meranda in the relay, too?" I didn't let her answer because the question was rhetorical, and I continued. "Why would she sabotage her own team?"

Liv looked at me, like a wounded animal and gasped.

"What would she have to gain?" I asked. It was possible that Liv could be right. She sat on my bed, and I did the same.

"I'm telling you; she is trying to take my place and push me out," Liv said, with her voice lowered. "You think I am just jealous and maybe I was at first, but I am serious. She is out to get me."

"But why though? She didn't even want to be in the coven. She didn't even know she was a witch at first," I tried to reason with her.

"Exactly! She doesn't know us. She doesn't care about us. She didn't even want to come here, and she's mad at her dad. She probably wants to entertain herself till she can figure out how to get back to Hawaii."

"Mrs. Wickstrom is so amazing, and she wouldn't lie to us. She and my grandmother were best friends their whole lives. She wouldn't encourage her granddaughter to join us if she is terrible," I said, laying back on my bed sideways and putting both hands on my forehead.

"SHE. DOESN'T. KNOW. HER." Liv said slowly and with anger. "She just met her, too, you know. Meranda is probably fooling her, too."

"Well, maybe you didn't touch the wall or maybe the official made a bad call. And I can't explain the invisible net, but there is no proof it was her," I said.

"I can't believe you would trust a stranger over me. We have been friends forever," Liv sobbed, and it tugged at my heart. "Mason finally talked to me, and it was obvious I like him. She's an empath, she knew what I was feeling, and she sent him away. She knew I was set to be team captain and she ripped it away from me. She didn't even try to say no. She just took it. Even joining the swim team, that was my thing. She knew it and took it all. I am water element, and she took that, too. Can't you just believe me for one second that she is out to destroy me?"

I sat up and stretched. I didn't blame Meranda for joining the swim team. She was on the team back in Hawaii and she was a swimmer her whole life. But it *was* kind of rude to accept the team captain position without even thinking of Liv and her feelings. It wasn't Meranda's fault if she was water element, but I didn't think she was. She was more. I believed she was the fifth element, or spirit. But Liv was right. We *didn't* know her. Her grandmother didn't know her either and she could be wrong about her, too. But I needed a full coven. I needed the missing witch to make us stronger so that I could successfully summon my grandmother.

"Maybe. But she's destined to join us. The fortune teller told us," I said in a last stitch effort to get Liv to try to make things work.

"We don't even know if that fortune teller was legit. She was at the county fair. Why do we need to be stronger? We can be stronger without another witch, we've been practicing and it's working," Liv said. I was going to lose her if I didn't fix this right then. I had to do something, say something.

"We need to be stronger than we can be without her," I said, tears welling up behind my eyes.

"WHY? Why her?"

"Because she's a Wickstrom witch and it was predicted that this generation would have a very powerful witch and she is the only one in her generation that has powers. We need her. *I* need her," I cried, the tears flowing freely as Liv appeared stunned. She didn't respond immediately and put her hands on her head.

"But why?" she finally asked, her voice softer.

"Because I *need* to summon my grandmother. I *need* to ask her something and every attempt I have made has failed," I admitted. Liv understood how much I loved my grandmother and although I didn't admit what I needed to ask her, she knew I was serious and that it was important. She hugged me long and hard.

"We can do this without her, you know. We don't need her. We can practice and get stronger and summon your grandma."

"I love you, Liv. You have been my best friend for years, but we need Meranda. I need the power of a Wickstrom witch! It needs to be her; can't you understand that?" I pleaded. "I need this!"

Liv seemed extremely upset and rose to her feet. She paced the room, and I could sense the internal conflict she was experiencing. She paused and faced me. Even though she wasn't saying anything, she was suddenly desperate to tell me something.

"What? What is it?" I asked, as I stood to face her. She put her hands on her forehead and breathed harder.

"*I'm* a Wickstrom witch.

Chapter 44

MERANDA

Some of my teammates said that Liv was yelling something about me and a net in the pool. Of course, that was ridiculous. I didn't do anything to her and nobody else believed I did anything either. At least, I didn't think so. The pool was checked because everyone saw her struggle, but nothing was found. I could've called or texted Liv to swear that I didn't do anything to her, but I left her alone instead.

Liv left with one of our teammates who got a ride from her parents, and I took the bus. I sat alone in the back and voice chatted with Bess.

"I swear I didn't do anything to her. Why would I?" I asked.

"I believe you, don't worry," Bess said, her glossed lips almost distracting me from my frustration.

"Do you think she made it up and accused me to try to make me look bad?" I asked, because at that point it was possible.

"No, I doubt it. I've known her pretty well for the last couple of years and she can be kind of bitchy, but I don't think she would lie to make you look bad."

"Great, so that means that she probably really thinks I did this, and she is going to convince Grace and Emily that I am out to get her," I glanced around the bus to make sure nobody was nearby or listening. "Do you think I should step down as captain?"

"No, of course not," she paused, and I sensed she wasn't telling me something.

"What?"

"Well, I mean. I don't want to upset you or anything. You deserved the captain position, of course, you did. I don't think you should quit, not at all. But... maybe you should have discussed it with Liv before accepting."

It was like I was stabbed in the chest. She thought I was wrong to take the captain position and I didn't want her to think negatively of me at all.

"Wow. Maybe I should just step down then. She can be captain, and everyone can be happy again," I said as tears stung my eyes. "I don't want to talk about it anymore because someone is going to hear."

"OK, but that isn't what I am saying. Call me when you get home. Meranda, I love you," she said before ending the video call. There it was again, that feeling in my chest. I was sad and feeling warm and fuzzy at the same time.

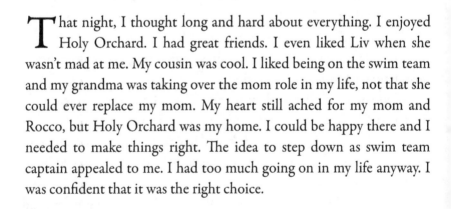

That night, I thought long and hard about everything. I enjoyed Holy Orchard. I had great friends. I even liked Liv when she wasn't mad at me. My cousin was cool. I liked being on the swim team and my grandma was taking over the mom role in my life, not that she could ever replace my mom. My heart still ached for my mom and Rocco, but Holy Orchard was my home. I could be happy there and I needed to make things right. The idea to step down as swim team captain appealed to me. I had too much going on in my life anyway. I was confident that it was the right choice.

Chapter 45
GRACE

I thought I misheard her, when Liv said she was a Wickstrom witch, but then she repeated herself. The confusion in my eyes must have been apparent.

"What do you mean *you* are a Wickstrom witch?"

"I will tell you everything, but I'm starving and exhausted," she said, sitting back down on my bed. "Can I stay the night?"

"Of course, I will get you some pajamas and we can order a pizza," the suspense was killing me, but Liv needed a friend right then and not me harassing her for information.

We both changed into pajamas and when the pizza came, we brought it up to my room. Wrapped in blankets on my bed, with the pizza between us, Liv admitted the secret she had been keeping.

"I'm a Wickstrom witch. Meranda's dad is my dad," she said, her eyes reflecting the pain she had been hiding.

"Holy moly! Are you sure?" I said, stunned and nearly choking on a slice of pizza.

"Remember when my mom went back into rehab this last time, in the summer?"

"Yeah," I was hanging on her every word.

"Well, I asked her why she never acted like my mom and why she couldn't stop doing drugs for me. She told me she knew who my dad was all along. And that he broke her heart and married someone else and had a family with her. He didn't care about us. So, she turned to drugs, and she just couldn't stop."

"Wow, so she told you it was Nate Wickstrom?" I was shocked and felt like I was watching a soap opera, starring my best friend.

"Not exactly. She refused to tell me who it was. I was so angry at her. But I went home and found her journals in the attic, from when she was a teen and young adult. She wrote about him. About how they were high school sweethearts until he moved to Boston to go to college, and they broke up. They had talked about her following him in a year and getting back together, but he met someone and got engaged."

"Well, that doesn't prove he's your father. He probably isn't because you and Liv were born on the same day. And based on how old your mother is and the age difference of Meranda and her father, you would have been born a few years before her."

"EXACTLY! He came back. He left his fiancé and came back for my mom. She wrote about it in one of her entries. They had a one-night stand and talked about picking up where they left off, but then he went back to Boston the next day and made up with *HER*!" Liv cried. There was more.

I moved the pizza to my nightstand and hugged her. My best friend was hurting and there was nothing I could do to help but try to comfort her.

"I was just a reminder of what my mom couldn't have. She didn't want me, but my grandma wouldn't let her give me up. She resented me, hated me. A souvenir of the day she found out the man she loved didn't want her," Liv cried harder.

"I don't think she hated you," I tried to reason with her.

"She wrote it in her journal. She said the words. She hated me. She didn't want me. And she told me that my dad didn't care about us. He had a different family."

"I'm so sorry for you, Liv. I can't believe you were holding this in. You could have told me from the beginning. I would have helped you through it," I said, as she laid down in my lap and I caressed the side of her face like a child.

"I couldn't. There's more," she said, sitting back up and clutching one of my pillows to her chest.

"What else? Does he know who you are?" I asked.

"I'll get to that. I found him on social media with his pictures of his perfect, beautiful family. Of *her*, the woman he chose over my mom and me. He had a daughter my age. I knew she would be a witch. So, when we went to visit the fortune teller and she talked about us being destined to have a powerful witch join our coven, I thought it could be her. I knew Mrs. Wickstrom still lived here. I knew that if we called for our lost witch and if it were her, that something, anything could bring her here," she squeezed the pillow so tight I thought the stuffing would pop out the seams.

"What is it? What are you trying to say, Liv?"

"You have to understand, I was out of my mind. I realized that week that both my parents wanted nothing to do with me and that the golden child who my dad chose over me, could possibly come here. I wanted her to stay away," she clenched her teeth as more tears and snot poured down her face. I grabbed her a tissue.

"What? What did you do?" Panic rose within me.

"I decided to kill her."

Chapter 46
MERANDA

Laying in my bed and staring at the ceiling, I was happy with my decision to step down from my role as captain of the swim team. I would announce it at the next meeting. I wasn't sure what they would do. Would there be a vote? Would Liv automatically become the new captain? I also wasn't sure if I should warn Liv.

As I was pondering all the questions I had in my mind, my vision became cloudy, and the ceiling merged with the walls and grew fuzzy. I went to sit up but found that I couldn't. I had no control of my muscles. I tried to move my arms, my legs, anything at all. Nothing would move. I tried desperately to close my eyes or at least blink but they wouldn't. I had no control over any part of my body, and it was terrifying. I tried to scream, but my mouth wouldn't open, and no sound would come from my vocal cords. Was I breathing? I couldn't tell, but I wasn't suffocating.

Then my eyes focused and there was a clear picture of what was in front of me... or on the ceiling? I was so confused as the white and brown blended and became more of a blue. I was staring out onto the ocean, then I glanced to the right. My mom helping Rocco onto our boat. *Wai nani.* It meant "beautiful water." Mom let me name our boat after my favorite thing. We bought it when I was twelve and she had just found out she was pregnant with Rocco.

My focus went from the boat to my mom and Rocco, and I was no longer aware of the fact that I was seeing all of this from my bedroom in Holy Orchard. It felt like I was there with them. I was stopped about thirty feet from the boat, looking down at my phone. Leilani had just texted telling me to have a great day with my family and I was responding.

"I will. I love u. Can't wait to see u tomorrow," I responded, *abbreviating only 'you' which Leilani always thought was weird.*

"Mana! Are you coming, or what?" Rocco yelled in his adorable toddler voice. I looked up and smiled.

"Of course, I'm coming! I wouldn't miss a day with you for the world!" I announced as I hurried toward the boat.

Rocco met me and reached up as I boarded the boat. I lifted him and squeezed him to my chest and reached out one arm to hug my mom. I had stayed the weekend at Leilani's, so I was very happy to see them again after two and a half days away.

"Where's Dad?" I asked, looking around, not able to detect him coming from the distance.

"He's not coming. Last minute golfing to try to hook a new client," she said, taking Rocco from me and getting his lime green life vest strapped onto him.

I could feel the disappointment followed by the scolding of myself for being surprised. Of course, he wasn't coming. Of course, he was golfing. He was always golfing. Always trying to hook a new client. I looked to Rocco and his smile had faded.

"It's okay Rocc! We are going to see some dolphins and whales. We are going to have a picnic and sing songs and it's okay that dad isn't here. Don't be sad," I said taking both of Rocco's hands.

"I'm sad Dad won't get to sing songs and see whales," Rocco said, frowning.

"Next time, baby," Mom said with her smile that could take away anyone's sadness.

WITCHES OF HOLY ORCHARD

"When can I golf?" Rocco asked.

"Next weekend, baby. Dad is going to teach you on Sunday," Mom said, and I was surprised.

I was suddenly aware that I was in some sort of memory or flashback. I forgot Dad was planning to teach Rocco to golf. There was a twinge in my chest and tears were burning the back of my eyes wanting to squeeze through, but I wouldn't let them. Dad was golfing a lot, but he still cared. As the flashback faded and my room came back into focus, memories of dad flashed before my eyes.

Dad made Rocco a pinata for his last birthday and showed him how to break it open with a stick while blind folded. I remember it was a dolphin because Rocco loved sea animals. Dad was artistic, too. It looked like a dolphin. Dad supervised play dates with Rocco and some of our parents' friends' kids, once a week.

Dad taught me to swim, to surf and to sail. Dad was around a lot when I was a kid and the first two years of Rocco's life, then something happened, and he was always golfing. He cared. I remembered that he cared but why was he always gone the last several months before the accident? Were Mom and Dad fighting? Planning a divorce? Was Dad cheating? I wanted to understand. Maybe I could've worked up the courage to ask him, but I was also afraid to hear the answer.

It made no sense because we had moved to Holy Orchard and he didn't have a job right away and he didn't even get the same job he had in Hawaii, but he was still always golfing. Maybe he cheated and he felt bad because Mom died? No matter what the answer was, I wasn't going to ask him that night. It was getting late, and my eyelids were heavy. It was time to sleep. I needed to deal with one issue at a time and the current one was stepping down as team captain. I would deal with what Dad was hiding later.

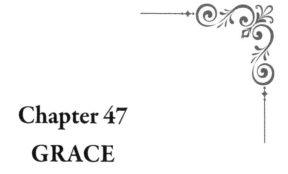

Chapter 47
GRACE

"What do you mean you decided to kill her? Who? Meranda?" I asked, shocked at what Liv had just told me.

"I was so filled with rage that I wanted Meranda to die. I didn't want her to come here, so I bought a couple of books on dark magic from the witchy shop, and I went home and studied them," Liv had her head down, but moved her eyes up to look at me. I let her continue, "When we did the ritual to call a lost witch, I summoned darkness and filled my object with my intentions for Meranda to die. I hated her. I wanted her to die."

"I can't believe you would think or do something so horrible," I said, my surprise and disappointment obvious in my voice. "What the HELL, Liv?"

"I was at my lowest point," Liv said, tears streamed quickly down her face. She reached her hand up to wipe them away, "But, I felt so guilty afterward. My chest was hurting, and it felt terrible to be so angry. I stayed up all night trying different spells and rituals to cancel it. I thought it worked, too because for two weeks, nothing happened. I asked Mrs. Wickstrom how she was doing every time she was at the cafe, and she didn't say anything about her granddaughter dying or getting hurt. I believed I was in the clear. Part of me hoped someone else would show up to be the missing witch."

"Do you know what this means? We really might have been responsible for the accident. For her mother and brother's deaths. We might have done this... show me what spells and rituals you did. Everything you did on your own without us. I need to know if we or you are responsible for this."

Liv was my best friend and I loved her. I knew her so well, but her confession made me realize maybe I didn't know her at all. She was someone who could try to kill someone, or use dark magic and possibly be successful at killing someone. There is no way that this was okay. I wanted to be supportive because my friend was hurting and she just confessed something huge to me, but I also wanted to push her out the door and tell her good luck in her life, but I wasn't going to be part of it. This was not forgivable. Lives were lost.

"I destroyed the book. I burned it right away after, but I think I can remember close to everything I did. I also did Internet searches to find things to try to cancel it. Give me a notebook and I will write everything down for you."

I watched her as she wrote, and I could sense the pain and regret she was feeling. At least she was sorry. She did try to cancel it. She was showing remorse, so maybe she could be forgiven. Maybe she wasn't even responsible. The idea popped into my head that if it had been so difficult to learn magic and fine tune her abilities, then how on Earth would she have been able to do some rituals from a book and make them happen? Especially something as difficult as controlling the weather across the planet and making almost three people die. It couldn't be possible.

Liv couldn't be responsible. Her revelation about being Meranda's sister was shocking. I was curious about so many things like what our next course of action should be. Liv continued to write, and I thought hard about whether we should tell Meranda or try to find out if Nate Wickstrom knows that he actually has *two* daughters.

Chapter 48
MERANDA

Waiting pool side, I watched my teammates file in from the locker rooms. Coach Melanie walked in last, holding her signature clipboard. I stood up and everyone sat on the edge of the pool, waiting for my daily pep talk. But instead of rattling off some inspirational quote I said I had an announcement to make. Coach Melanie glared at me, puzzled since I didn't fill her in on my plans prior. I looked to Liv, and she stared up at me with a glossy sadness to her eyes. What was she thinking? Taking a deep breath and realizing I needed to just say it fast, or I never would, I blurted it out.

"I'm stepping down from my position as team captain, effective immediately," I said quickly, as Mason Hartley lost his balance and fell into the pool. Suddenly the voices of the entire team talking at once echoed and bounced off the walls of the natatorium. Coach Melanie blew her whistle and the voices stopped.

"What are you talking about?" she asked.

"There are other people more deserving of the position. I shouldn't have even agreed to take it when it was offered. Everyone here knows it. It was handed to me, and I should have declined," I said as Coach Melanie tried to speak. I raised my voice, continuing to talk over her, "I have really enjoyed being the team captain and I hope you all can forgive me. May the more deserving person step up and be our captain."

"Everyone, swim laps, I need to talk to Meranda!" Coach Melanie shouted, her voice cracking as she directed me away from the pool. "Why are you doing this?" she asked, only to me.

"Please make Liv the team captain. She worked so hard for it and if I hadn't come along, she would have gotten the position. You can't deny that," I said fiercely. "There's no one better fit than her."

"You're right, but she's got a lot to learn when it comes to being a team leader," Coach said, her arms crossed as she lowered her eyebrows at me.

"So, work with her on that. She could be amazing if you give her the chance and she wants it. She deserves it. *I* don't. Just give it to her, please. I'm not afraid to quit the team if that is what it takes," I threatened.

"No, no. Don't even think about that. Ugh. You put me in a situation that I don't want to be in right now, Meranda, but I don't want you to quit the team. Please don't," she said, blowing into her whistle again. The team finished their last laps and got out of the pool, sitting on the edge looking up at Coach Melanie.

"After speaking with Meranda, I accept her resignation. However, I need a day or two to decide on a replacement. There are forms in my office for anyone who is interested in applying as team captain. We're cutting practice early today, so you are dismissed. See you tomorrow."

I glanced over at Liv, and she lowered her eyebrows and frowned deeply at me. She was angry? Incredibly angry. What the Hell? She should be excited about this. Everyone filed into the locker rooms and Coach asked me to hang back for a minute. By time I got into the locker room, Liv was already leaving.

I skipped the shower since I never did get into the pool, and I dressed faster than I had in my life. I ran down the hall and out the doors in time to notice Liv heading down the street. I jogged quickly after her and caught up to her as she was crossing the street.

"Wait! Liv!" I yelled as she continued walking.

"Just, STOP. I can't even wrap my head around all this. What are you even trying to do?" she turned to face me.

"I'm trying to make things better. I want to stay in Holy Orchard," I said.

"STOP!" she yelled and walked faster down the street.

"Where are you going? You don't live that way?" I shouted.

"None of your business."

I stopped and stood on the corner of the street and let her walk away. There were cars driving by and people staring. I didn't want to look like a crazy stalker person. She was walking toward my house. She was probably going to Grace's.

I continued to walk home keeping half a block of distance between Liv and me. I was right. I watched her go up to Grace's door and knock, then she walked in. I speed walked the rest of the way and passed by my own house to go to Grace's. I knocked on the door, then walked in, too. Grace and Liv were arguing in her room. As I crept up the stairs, I overheard what they were saying.

"I think we should tell her," Grace said.

"No, we shouldn't. We shouldn't EVER tell her. Maybe she will go back to Hawaii," Liv said. They clearly didn't hear me knock and had no idea I was there. I sat at the top of the stairs and listened, even though it felt wrong.

"You are sisters. Maybe once she knows you can act like sisters. You could form an unbreakable bond. She doesn't even understand your connection to her."

"No and don't you dare try to tell her. I will seriously hate you forever if you go behind my back and tell her," Liv shouted angrily with desperation in her voice.

171

"I won't. I wouldn't ever do that, and I'm shocked that you would think I would. I am just saying I think she should know, and I think we or you should tell her. I wouldn't ever go behind your back and tell her. Geeze."

There was mostly silence and the slight sound of heavy breathing and movement. They were no longer talking, and I was trying to process what I just heard. It made no sense. What did Grace mean about being sisters? Did she mean like sister witches? Sisters in the coven? Because we weren't actual sisters. I got up the nerve to go in and ask them.

Stomping hard on the top of the stairs to make sure they knew I was there and an attempt to convince them I just arrived, I walked loudly to Grace's bedroom and knocked on the door frame. Her door was already open. They both looked like they had just seen a ghost as I walked in.

"Hey," I said, pretending I heard nothing. "Did you hear? I stepped down as team captain."

"Oh...uh. Yeah. Liv told me. We were just talking about it. I think it's nice that you did that, but it doesn't mean you didn't deserve to be captain," Grace said. I could feel her heartbeat speeding up. She was nervous and so was Liv. They were nervous *and* afraid. I was sure they wondered if I had heard them. They weren't talking about sister witches or sisters in the coven. They were talking about something else. Goosebumps polka-dotted my arms and all my hairs stood up.

"What else were you talking about?" I asked, suspiciously.

"Nothing," Liv said, as she tried to push past me to leave.

"Grace?" I asked, blocking Liv's path out the door. "What did I overhear?"

"You were listening to our private conversation? What is wrong with you?" Liv asked.

"I want to know what you are hiding because I am an empath, and you know I can sense what you are both feeling right now. You are hiding something. I am not going to let this go."

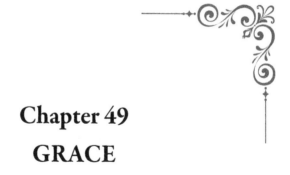

Chapter 49
GRACE

Meranda could sense that Liv and I were hiding something. She overheard part of our conversation. If there was ever a time to tell her, that was it, but I promised Liv I wouldn't ever tell. Meranda deserved to know, and I genuinely believed that they could become closer if only she knew. I stared at Liv and tried to convince her with my eyes. She glared back at me.

Meranda stood firm in the doorway and wouldn't let Liv pass by her.

"I will knock you over if you don't move and let me out," Liv said through her clenched teeth.

"You don't have anywhere to be. Practice got done early and we would normally still be there right now. You also don't work at the cafe tonight, so we have all the time in the world to discuss this," Meranda said. I was surprised because I never heard her talk like that. She sounded so brave and not wounded like she normally was.

"There's nothing to discuss, but I want out of here."

"What were you two saying about me?" Meranda asked, looking from Liv to me.

"I don't know what you THINK you heard, but we weren't talking about anything except you stepping down as captain and practice getting done early," Liv said, balling up her fists.

"You said something about sisters. What's that about," Meranda asked, accusingly. It was a good time to tell her, but it still couldn't be me, so I grabbed Liv's shoulder and looked her sternly in the eyes.

"Tell her. She has a right to know," I said, followed by Liv giving me a betrayed look.

"See? I knew it. Tell me what?" Meranda asked.

"Fine! Your dad screwed my mom and then she had me, so guess that means he's my dad, too and we are sisters," Liv turned to me, "I officially hate you now, Grace." Liv pushed Meranda out of the way and stormed out of the house, leaving me with Meranda to fill in the blanks. I was heartbroken because she said she hated me. Liv was my best friend, and she was angry and hurting. But Meranda was my friend, too and Mrs. Wickstrom's granddaughter. I still believed something good could come from it.

Chapter 50
MERANDA

My dad was hiding something. I had to confront him because there were so many questions in my mind. When Liv and Grace told me that Liv was my sister, I wasn't surprised. Dad was acting different for months before the accident, then we moved to Holy Orchard. He was always golfing. Why? Did my mom know about any of this? Did she die knowing her husband had a kid with another woman? Or was she kept in the dark like I was? Did Grandma know? It was hard deciding who to confront first. Grandma was usually home and more available to me, but Dad... I needed to know more what *he* knew.

Dad was working late that night, but I would wait up to talk to him. Grandma questioned me when I was sitting in the living room facing the door like a parent waiting to catch their child sneaking in after dark. I told her I wanted to wait up so I could talk to Dad about something, and she didn't press me for more information. I loved her for that.

At 11:23 PM, Dad's key rattled in the door's lock. I dug my nails hard into the arms of the chair I was sitting in, and I took a deep breath. As Dad walked in, I stared hard, almost through him.

"Hey Mana, what you doing up so late, Sweetie?"

"Don't call me that," I said.

"Mana or sweetie?" Dad asked.

"Mana, that was *his* name for me. I told you already," I said, getting sidetracked.

"Sorry, Sweetie. I will try to do better. What are you doing up so late?"

"I heard some interesting information about you, today, Dad," I said, as Dad walked in and set his things down on the little table in the hallway. I didn't sense any emotional change in him. I didn't hear his heartbeat speed up or anything.

"Do you want to go talk in the kitchen? We can have some tea?" Dad asked and I shook my head in agreement.

"I will boil some water; will you get out a couple teacups?" Dad asked. It was strange. He wasn't worried. He also didn't seem curious about what I was going to ask him. "What kind of tea do you want?"

"Hibiscus," I said. "Should I grab one for you, too?"

Dad nodded and reached for the cherry streusel Grandma had made, cutting a piece for each of us.

"So, what did you hear at school that was so interesting about me?"

"It wasn't at school. I heard it at Grace's house. Remember my friend Liv?"

"Ah, LeAnne's daughter?" Dad said fondly.

"Umm, I don't know her name. But Liv is one of my friends from school. She's Grace from next door? Her best friend. Anyway, she had interesting things to say about you, today, and I wanted to know if they were true," I asked, braver as every second passed.

"I think they're true," he said calmly, pouring the hot water over each of our tea bags.

"You think they're true? Do you even understand what I am talking about?" I asked, getting frustrated.

"I think so. Yeah." It was like neither one of us wanted to say the words, so I summoned the bravery from inside me.

"Is Liv your daughter?" I stated it as a question, rather than an accusation, trying to give him the chance to explain. He took a deep breath.

"She probably is," he said, and I was finally able to sense a change in his emotion. Sadness maybe. His heart was beating faster, too. After several moments of waiting for him to say more, the frustration built up inside me.

"Hello? Explain please?" I said, squeezing my tea bag with the back of my spoon, making it bleed across the hot water in my cup.

"How much do you know?" he asked, doing the same to his tea bag.

"How about you start from the beginning, Dad."

"I dated LeAnne in high school. We were together for four years. I was a grade ahead of her in school. We planned to get married, but I went to college, and I met your mom. I loved LeAnne. She was familiar and all I had ever known. She was safe. But your mom, she was exotic and mysterious. I fell hard for her, fast."

"That's lovely," I said, sarcastically.

"Your mom and I were together for years and had just gotten engaged. She wanted to go back home to Hawaii to do her residency there and she asked me to marry her and go with her. I got scared."

"So, you cheated on Mom?" I asked, although I didn't think he did, but I wanted to torture him a little.

"No, never. We broke up. I don't even remember why. Something stupid and we called the engagement off. I went home to Holy Orchard and the first person I ran into was LeAnne. She was safe and familiar. It was good to be with her again and we picked up right where we left off. We talked about getting married."

That was not the right thing to say to me, that my dad wanted to be with another woman other than my mom. My dead mom. My anger turned to tears and my lip quivered in protest. My bravery grew wings and flew out the window.

"Sweetie, don't cry."

"I'm not," I insisted.

"I loved your mother more than anything and I regretted leaving as soon as my anger and adrenaline from the fight wore off. Then she called me and asked me to come back to school. Long story short, we worked things out and I never saw LeAnne again."

"So, you didn't know? But you found out somehow? When?" I took a sip of my tea and burnt my tongue. "Ow," I said putting it down and pushing it aside.

"When you were born, a mutual friend of mine and LeAnne told me how crazy it was that LeAnne just had a baby on the same day. I did the math and decided the baby *could* be mine, so I called her," Dad took a spoon of tea and blew on it before taking a sip, clearly learning from my mistake.

"She insisted that she was on birth control when she was with me and that she got off it a couple of months later when she met her new boyfriend, that the baby was premature. I told her I wanted a DNA test to be sure and she called me every name in the book. She said her boyfriend was the father and I needed to drop it. I trusted her to tell me the truth, so I dropped it. Plus, I was all the way in Hawaii, and it would have been harder to fight. And maybe she was telling the truth. Probably she was."

"Dad, then she probably isn't. She would have told you then so she could get child support or something. She probably lied to Liv or Liv is lying now," I said, hopeful.

"No, that's unfortunately not the end of the story. LeAnne, I guess didn't take our breakup too well and turned to drugs. She blamed me after her new boyfriend ditched her. But I was all the way in Hawaii enjoying life. I didn't know anything that was going on with her. Our mutual friends had lost touch with both of us. I didn't hear anything from or about her until last year."

"What happened last year?" I asked, blowing on my tea, and taking a guarded sip.

"LeAnne got a hold of me and said her daughter was my daughter. She demanded $100,000 or she would blow up my life. Even if it weren't true, it would still make me look bad. She threatened your mom and you and Rocco. I had to pay it."

"You gave that crazy woman $100,000??" I said loudly as the floor creaked upstairs. Oops. I woke up Grandma.

"Yes, at first, I hid it from your mom. I couldn't just take the money out of our account because she would notice. So, I took out a loan."

"For $100,000?" I whispered. "I didn't know they had loans that high."

"It was through my company. That is why it was so important for me to hook those big clients. I needed the money to pay it back. But I was also struggling hard with the idea that I might have a daughter out there raised by a drug addict. I hired a private investigator who was willing to take risks. I found out that she was being raised by her grandma and doing well. I still needed to know, so I had him get some of her DNA. I didn't ask how he got it, but he did. We had it tested, and it said it was 97 point something percent that we were biologically related as parent and child."

"Oh dang. Did Mom ever know?" I asked, taking a sip of my tea as the exhaustion set in.

"Yes, the weekend before the accident when you stayed at Leilani's. I told her what I had been hiding. I couldn't keep it hidden from her. I needed her support, and she was amazing. We talked about moving to Holy Orchard so I could fight for my daughter. We knew you would be upset to leave Leilani and your home, but you would love your grandma and you'd have a new sister. Then the accident happened."

"Did Grandma know?" I asked, suddenly more upset.

"I'd been in touch with her before the accident. We had made plans for all of us to move in. But no, I planned to tell her after we arrived."

"Does she know now?"

"No, not from me anyway. If she knows she found out some other way."

"Dad, we have been here three months already! Why didn't you tell me or Grandma or try to see Liv? So much time has passed since you found out. Liv has only gotten more and more angry and mean because she has known about you for months and thinks you chose your other family over her. She hates me because of you!" I ended up shouting again and Grandma's footsteps tapped louder as she made her way down the stairs.

"I was trying to work and pay back the money and I was trying to track down LeAnne. I haven't been able to get a hold of her and nobody knows where she is. I also didn't think Liv knew anything about me. I wasn't sure how to approach it. Plus, I was grieving the loss of my wife and son and everything we had planned for our future," Dad put his head in his hands and cried, just as Grandma walked into the room.

"What on Earth is happening in this kitchen?"

Chapter 51
LIV

Screw friends. I didn't have any friends. I didn't have any parents, or siblings. The only person in the world who cared about me was my grandma. And I made her life harder. Sure, I helped at the cafe, but she didn't ask for any of this. She didn't plan to raise another kid after her own kids were grown and out of the house. She should have been enjoying retirement but instead she was working herself to death running the cafe so that she could afford to take care of me.

I wasn't sure where I was going as I packed everything I could fit into my duffel bag, but I needed to get away. Maybe out of Holy Orchard, maybe out of Massachusetts. I would even probably leave the East side of the country. California was supposed to be nice.

I pulled the dusty lock box from under my bed and used the small key on my HOH Swim key chain to open it. I had my birth certificate, social security card and $536. I took it all and shoved it between my socks and underwear in my duffel bag.

Chapter 52
GRACE

After everything came out about Meranda and Liv being sisters, neither one of them would talk to me. Liv said she hated me as she stormed out of my house. I tried calling and texting her and she didn't answer. She also wasn't in school. Meranda told me she didn't hate me, but she really needed time to work through things with her father and grandmother.

I was worried about Liv, but I needed to focus on making the coven stronger. We were down two witches, so that meant we needed to focus on making the three of us stronger. I called an emergency coven meeting for the three of us, at my house. When Bess and Emily arrived, we sat down on the floor of my room and casted a circle around us.

"Has anyone heard from Liv?" I asked, glancing from Bess to Emily.

"No. Nothing," Bess said.

"Me neither, what's going on?" Emily asked. Of course, Bess would know because she and Meranda were dating. If Emily hadn't heard from Liv, then she really didn't know anything.

"Well, it's an awfully long story, but for time's sake I am going to give you the condensed version. Pretty much, Liv found out that Nate Wickstrom was her father and that is why she had been hating on Meranda so much. Meranda stepped down as captain of the swim team. Liv got mad, though I have no idea why, then Liv and I were arguing about telling Meranda that Liv is her sister and she overheard. Liv hates me because she blames me for Meranda finding out. Now Liv is not answering our calls and hasn't been in school. Meranda is taking some time to deal with things with her family. So, it's just the three of us for now."

"Oh, my Goddess! Am I the last to know?" Emily asked, appalled.

"It seems so," Bess said.

"So, I think we should continue working on getting stronger in our abilities. Do you agree?" I asked, looking to Bess and Liv.

"Yes," Bess said.

"I'm in," Emily said.

"I think we should work on Emily's abilities first. Bess, you are already doing well with yours. Try to focus on swirling larger objects for longer amounts of time. Emily, how far have you gotten with your solo practice?" I asked.

"I'm still trying to start larger fires and keep them burning. I can light small flames like candles. I can melt things like ice and chocolate, but nothing major like metal. I've been trying though. I've also been working on trying to communicate with animals, but I don't know how it works. Am I supposed to read their minds? Or will they talk and only I can hear it?"

"I think you will possibly be able to read their minds, but they will also speak to you in their language, like cats meowing. And you should just understand what it means," I said.

"Oh, that's interesting, but I don't know if I will be able to do it. Is there anything you want me to work on more?" Emily asked.

"Hmm, I'm not sure. Do you feel like you are stronger when you are angry or during moments of passion?" I asked.

"Passion? What do you mean?" Emily asked, giggling.

"I mean, like if you are making out with Dean, do you feel more in control or out of control of your powers? Like would you be able to ignite a fire or melt something if you were having a moment of passion?"

"Wow, it just got really uncomfortable in here," Bess said.

"No, we are all friends. We are all girls. We can talk about this stuff. Yeah, I think so. I was afraid the other day when we were kissing, I thought my skin was going to burn him," Emily said.

"Ooooo, maybe his skin is fire resistant because of his Wickstrom witch blood?" Bess said as Emily smacked her in the arm. I made a mental note that we needed to find out if Dean had any of that Wickstrom witch power.

"This is great to hear. I think we should work on trying to melt things and create bigger fires. Communicating with animals would be nice, but I think it shouldn't be our immediate focus. When you do try it, you can borrow Tinkerbell," I said.

"You might find it beneficial to do that ritual that me and Meranda did, you know, the journey to find your spirit animal," Bess chimed in.

"Yeah, I think I might, but for now I just want to burn and melt things," Emily said clenching her right fist and smiling deviously.

"You are too funny," I said, but I was happy she was so enthusiastic. With Meranda and Liv currently out of the picture, my best hope of making the coven stronger was with Emily's fire powers.

I had waited so long to communicate with my grandmother and all my attempts had been failed. However, each time I did it, I was closer to being able to make it work. I was confident that if I had Bess and Emily, at least, stronger in their powers combined with mine, we could summon my grandmother.

"I have an idea; we should meet after school every day this week and work on trying to burn and melt things. Collect all the scrap metal that you can find, and we will bring it out to that abandoned shack in the woods. We can use the fire ring there and try to melt the metal. Also, if there is anything you want to burn, bring that, too. I will tell you the time to meet and whether we are meeting there or here. Any questions?"

"No, but I have a few things I want to burn and melt. I'm excited," Bess said, clapping her hands.

"No questions from me, Boss. It's about time I get some attention around here," Emily said, possibly joking, but I couldn't tell. I made a mental note to pay more attention to Emily just in case she really was feeling neglected.

"Alright then, it's a plan."

Chapter 53
MERANDA

For some reason, my dad felt the need to keep secrets from me all the time. I didn't know anyone in his family existed until a few months prior. I didn't know I had a sister my whole life. Literally, my whole life because she was born the same day as me. All the secrets. All the lies. I hated him for lying to me, but he was still my dad and I loved him. It was a strange feeling to hate someone and love them at the same time.

I didn't completely understand why he kept my grandma, my aunts and uncles, and cousins a secret from me. Sure, Grandma was a little eccentric and maybe a little crazy, but he was so quick to run to her when his life was falling apart. She was obviously important and a source of comfort to him. So why would he have ever left?

Maybe there was something real about Wickstrom witches being susceptible to dark magic, like the stories told. Did he know I was a witch and that I had powers? Was he trying to protect me by keeping me from my birthright? Maybe they had a fight, and he was too prideful to admit he was wrong. Maybe *she* was wrong, and it took him way too long to forgive her. I didn't want to be angry at someone my whole life and vowed to never hold a grudge.

Grandma told me the first week I was in Holy Orchard that there were old journals and books written about my ancestors. There were copies and originals in her library downstairs. I laid in my bed unable to think of anything else. I had flipped through some of the pages when I first moved here, but now I was curious what else they said. It was more than curiosity. I *needed* to read them. I remembered the information I already learned from talking to my grandma and from briefly reading through some of the books in the library.

My ancestor Elizabeth Ferris was believed to have used dark magic to make Mayor Wickstrom fall in love with her and spare her life during the witch trials in the 1600s. The stories that were passed down say that her children were born from dark magic and every Wickstrom witch had a little bit of it in them from birth. It took extra effort to be good. All I could think about was reading those books and finding out more about my ancestry. I couldn't just get up and go into Grandma's library. It was 2 AM. I tried to close my eyes, to sleep, but it was like I drank an energy drink.

My head pounded and my stomach ached. My eyes were dry, but I still couldn't keep them closed long enough to sleep. My ancestors were nagging at me. I could almost hear them telling me to sneak downstairs and read the stories. I cursed myself for not reading them sooner. I had been there for months. Why didn't I try to read them sooner? My family history was kind of important, especially after finding out I had a whole family my dad had kept from me.

First, I laid in bed waiting for time to pass, but every time I glanced at my watch only a few minutes had passed. Sleep or wait? Sleep or wait? I couldn't sleep, but my mind wouldn't let me wait. I crept out of my room, down the hall and I made my footsteps as light on the stairs as I possibly could. I was barely breathing as to not wake my dad or grandma. I walked across the Victorian furniture in the living room and found the door to the library in the dark.

When I turned the light on, the books were sitting out on the table in the middle of the room. Just waiting for me, like they knew I was coming for them. The leather-bound cover was bumpy against my fingers, as I ran them across the book on the top. That book was written by Dorothy Wickstrom, my grandmother's grandmother. Not too many generations back, but she was long dead already. I could have brought the stack to my bedroom, but I sat in the library and read them there instead. There would be less chance of getting caught if I read them there. Err, maybe caught was the wrong word. It wasn't like I was doing anything wrong. I was just up in the middle of the night reading about my ancestry. That was a completely normal and levelheaded thing to do.

I sat down at the table and focused on the stack of books. Dorothy Wickstrom's book was calling out to me, so I started with that one. I read it cover to cover before the sun came up, right there in the library. Dorothy wrote of the stories she read about in our ancestors' journals that have since been destroyed or are no longer readable. She also wrote about the stories that were passed down by word of mouth. She spoke of a curse.

No Wickstrom witch shall have ever lasting love. Those who try find heartache when death claims victory on their beloved. I gasped aloud when I read that part. Dorothy wrote about losing her beloved Henry to a drowning accident three days before their wedding was supposed to take place. My heart plummeted in my chest. My mom and Rocco. Dad's beloved. My grandpa Sam. Grandma's beloved. Both of my aunts lost their husbands. There was a trend. Could there really be a curse? It was plausible based on the evidence.

AMY SOUTHARD

There were six more books and I flipped through them all quickly just to get an idea of what they were. Dad would have been up soon to get ready for work and Grandma wouldn't be far behind him. There was a small, newer looking handwritten journal. It was pages and pages of names and dates. There was a creak at the top of the stairs alerting me that someone was up. I tucked the book under my arm inside my pajamas and sneaked out to the kitchen, prepared to make up some lie about getting up for a snack.

When several minutes passed and nobody had come down, I sneaked back up the stairs and into my room where I finally examined the book more closely. It resembled Grandma's handwriting and it was a list of every person in the Wickstrom family, starting with Elizabeth Ferris and ending with Rocco. Next to everyone's name was written either another name and a date, or the word "single." Next to Rocco's name "single" was written. Next to mine was blank. Next to Dad's name was my mom's name and the date of the accident.

My stomach churned as the acid rose to my throat. There were hundreds of names, few were "single" and most had a name and date written next to it. I turned what I thought was the last page that was written on, because Rocco's name was on the bottom and there was something written on the first line on the back. "Olivia 'Wickstrom' Olsen." Blank. No name or date next to it. Olivia Wickstrom Olsen was Liv. The ink was not fresh. Grandma knew. How long did she know?

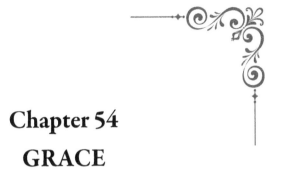

Chapter 54
GRACE

Concern for Liv overcame me quite a few times, but one thing was true. Liv and I always made up. Things always worked out. Liv was angry at me and out doing who knows what, but there was no time to waste. I needed to talk to my grandmother. I needed to summon her and if Liv and Meranda weren't available, I wasn't going to wait for them.

There was probably little to no chance that Bess, Emily and I would have been powerful enough to do a summoning spell on our own but making our powers stronger wouldn't have hurt. If anything, it would have made it easier for us to summon her once Meranda and Liv got their stuff together and rejoined us.

Liv was most likely safe and completely fine wherever she was. Her grandmother Ruth must have known where she was because she hadn't called me to ask if I knew where she was. The thought calmed my nerves as I searched through boxes in my garage. I was trying to find things for Emily to melt and burn with her powers.

The old red wagon I used to pull my dolls and stuffed animals in as a child sat in the corner, unused for nearly a decade. It was turned over on its side and when I flipped it back on its wheels, a large spider skittered out.

"Oh hello, friendly spider, do you have a message for me?" I asked as it stopped and stared up at me with its eight eyes. My grandmother always told me that anytime a spider surprises you, she has a message for you. I never did learn how to receive the messages, so I was always asking spiders what they were and getting no response. I made a mental note to research that further when I had the time.

I filled the wagon with anything I believed would melt or burn that no longer served a purpose. Old wooden handles to brooms, shovels, and rakes. Grandmother always kept them because "you never know when you might need something to stake up a tomato plant or hold a fence in place." Maybe I didn't know if I would need them someday, but I didn't need them then. They would have better served me and the coven by burning. In the wagon, they went.

When I moved a board that had been resting against the wall, the head of a spaded shovel fell and clanked against the concrete floor of the garage. Hmm... I had many wooden handles, but I wanted to burn them. I could have saved one and attached the head, but it was rusted, and it was metal. It would melt. I tossed the rusty head into the wagon.

As I searched for wood and metal scraps, I thought of my Grandmother Sophie. The whole reason for my efforts. The reason for all of it. I needed to see her one last time, to ask her a final question, something that burned inside me. Ever since my grandmother passed away, the question nagged at me. She died without giving me the one answer I needed the most. I tried but I couldn't let it go. I needed to know.

There were times when I wondered if it was all worth it. The coven existed already before she died. Of course, I didn't create the coven to get answers. My grandmother, Liv's grandmother Ruth and Mrs. Wickstrom were all in a coven with three other women, from when they were young girls. Liv and I always looked up to them and we were inspired. We craved the magic and were eager to learn. Witches of Holy Orchard was born with its founding two members, then we added Emily and later Bess. We believed four was enough until we spoke with the fortune teller at the county fair and found out we were destined to add a fifth. Meranda.

We were excited and in awe of the magic in everything around us. But when my grandmother died, it became something more. Something I needed and was desperate for. I was constantly needing to be stronger and more powerful because every attempt at summoning my grandmother was failed. The question poked at me at all hours of the day and night. It was active in my dreams. It showed up in pictures. It lingered in the shadows and watched over my shoulder. It was in every flower in the garden and in the face of every animal at the shelter. Escape was not possible, not that I wanted to. It was simple. She only needed to tell me, to speak the words.

I tried using a talking board, I tried listening to the wind. Reading tea leaves never amounted to anything. Tarot cards were fun but didn't answer my question. I needed my grandmother to speak the words. I needed to summon her and that was the only solution. So, in short, yes, my efforts were worth it. And even though my reasons were selfish, the coven would thank me when they benefited, too. Stronger, more powers, confidence. They were going to get something out of it. Knowing that made it so much easier to do what I was going to do next.

I found a metal ladder hanging in the garage. It was old and I couldn't remember ever seeing anyone use it. I could bring it to melt, although it was longer than my wagon. I pulled it off the hooks that were holding it up and turned it on its side. I could use it for something. It was a bit rusted but would probably look nice in the flower garden as a decoration. Maybe Mrs. Wickstrom would find use of it. I gently lifted it back onto its hooks and continued searching for more items to burn and melt.

When I turned around, I knocked over a 2x4 that was leaning against the wall and noticed a shelf peeking out behind it. There was a black box with a lock on it and the key was inside. I stood on my tippy toes to reach the box and pull it down to the workbench nearby. I wasn't sure who it belonged to or what was inside, but the key was in it. That was invitation enough for me to open it and be nosy.

I turned the key and lifted the lid to find a bunch of baby items. Aww... They were my mother's baby items. I found a little pink t-shirt with a picture of a stork and the words *I met my mother at Holy Orchard General Hospital*. That was adorable. There was a rattle, a baby hairbrush, a lock of blond hair and what appeared to be an umbilical cord stump. *Eww*. There was a card with her name from the hospital that had a baby footprint on it and there were several pictures from when she was a newborn. There was a picture of two babies. I turned it over and read the back. *Elizabeth and Sarah- 1 week and 2 weeks old. The day before she died.*

It was Grandmother's handwriting and she had drawn a sad face next to the words. I felt so bad for Mrs. Wickstrom. I could just imagine what life would have been like if Sarah had lived. My mother and Sarah would have probably grown up as best friends. Maybe Sarah would have had kids my age. Maybe a son that I could have fallen in love with. The boy next door. I was picturing it and thinking of how great it could have been, but also sad that Mrs. Wickstrom had to lose a child. I wouldn't have wished that on my worst enemy.

My phone chimed that I had a text. It was a group text with Bess and Emily and Bess had asked if we were ready to meet yet. The text snapped me out of my daydream, and I needed to hurry. I replied in the group text that I was almost done, then I locked the box and put it back on its shelf. Time to set stuff on fire.

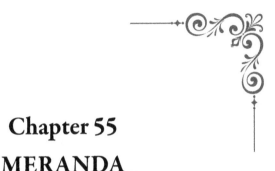

Chapter 55
MERANDA

After school, I was supposed to have swim team practice, but I blew it off. Talking to my grandma was way more important. I walked up the sidewalk to grandma's house. *My house.* The front of the house was so inviting, and I thought of how the door and windows made it look like a face. It was almost like the house was smiling at me.

I clutched the small book that was written in my grandma's cursive and held it to my chest. I had questions and wanted answers. Inhaling deeply as I walked in the door, the smell of slow cooked pot roast and vegetables invited me in.

"Grandma?" I called out. There was no response, so I called out louder, then stopped to listen. There was a creaking upstairs, but she didn't come down. I took a deep breath then started to yell, "Grra..." I was cut off.

"Hey, Sweetie. Grandma is out with some friends." My dad's voice called out from the upstairs bathroom.

I had gone planning to confront my grandma about how long she had known about Liv being a Wickstrom, but my dad was home in the late afternoon for once. I had an opportunity to talk to him about what he knew about witches, dark magic, and my own powers. Did he have powers? Did he know I had them? Why did he really keep me from my grandma? There was so much I wanted to know, and I also just missed him.

"Hey, Dad. Can we talk?" I yelled up to him, a twinge in my gut. Maybe I would lose my nerve.

My dad came walking down the stairs wearing blue jeans and a black shirt. He was barefoot and drying his hair with a white towel. My heart was pounding. If he ran away to Hawaii because he thought Grandma was crazy for all the witchy stuff she did and talked about, he would probably disown me if I told him I had actual powers.

"What do you want to talk about?" he asked, motioning me to the living room. We sat in Grandma's matching blue Victorian chairs as I struggled to find the confidence to say what I wanted to say. Finally, it was time to just blurt it out.

"What do you know about magic... and the Wickstrom witches?" I asked. Dad hesitated for a moment, then adjusted himself in his chair.

"Everything. All of it."

I wasn't expecting this answer, but I also didn't believe it.

"Dad... I doubt it. Tell me what you know. I need specifics."

"I'm sure you haven't forgotten who your grandma is? She is my mom, and I grew up with her. I spent almost two decades in her house," he dried his hair a little more by rubbing the towel vigorously over his head as he waited for me to say something.

"Well, yeah of course, I know who grandma is. I know she was your mom first. But that doesn't answer my question, Dad," I said, as I got a little frustrated and had a bit of a tone when I said the word "dad."

"Okay, well I know the history of the Wickstrom family about Mayor Wickstrom and his servant who is believed to have used dark magic to get him to fall in love with her. I know about witches and having powers and I am guessing you wonder if I know anything about you and your abilities," he stopped talking and rolled his towel up super tight until it was a small roll in his hands.

"Uh, yeah. So do you have any powers?" I asked.

Dad smiled and seemed to think about what he said first.

"Do you? Dad?"

"Well, kind of but not exactly," he said.

"What does that mean? Kind of but not exactly?"

"Sometimes I can sense things coming on. Almost like a bad feeling if something bad will happen or a good feeling if something good is going to happen. I had a good feeling the days you and your brother were born, for example. The day of the accident I had a bad feeling. But I guess people who aren't witches have that, too, sometimes."

"I guess. Is there anything else you can do? What element are you attuned to?"

"Fire. But my powers were just passive. Like I said, sensing things. Prophetic dreams. But I have always been just a normal guy. There was just the one thing," Dad smiled.

"What is it?" I asked, leaning forward to hear more.

"The power to tell awesome dad jokes," Dad said, laughing.

"Oh my gosh, Dad, I'm being serious right now," I said, although his laugh was contagious, and I smiled a little.

"Well, I can communicate with animals. It's really the only fire element power I ever had. And it wasn't something I could just do at will. Usually, I will be sitting minding my own business and a bird will land next to me and say something rude. I never really practiced trying to get better at it."

"Cool. You should practice. It could be useful someday," I said, impressed that he had a power. At least he would probably be open minded about me having abilities. Even though he would probably not freak out, I was still nervous to tell him.

"Do you know that *I* have powers?" I asked. My heart pounded as I waited for his answer. Time was passing in slow motion as I counted every heartbeat until he answered.

"Of course. Grandma and I talk about you. You are in a coven, and you have been practicing your magic, learning to do some spells and you have some special abilities."

"What abilities, Dad? Do you know what I can do?"

"I know you can feel and sometimes control other people's emotions. Grandma told me. I know that you can visit the past in your dreams."

"What else?" I asked as I dug my fingernails into the palms of my hands. I was getting frustrated.

"Okay Meranda, why don't you just tell me what you want me to know. I can tell you are getting upset and we are just wasting time with this." His words stung a little and I was wounded. He rarely ever used that tone with me, and I briefly remembered being *Daddy's Little Girl*. I was probably unintentionally controlling his emotions.

"Do you know that I can breathe under water?" He seemed surprised. He probably didn't know, so I continued. "I can breathe under water. While I am swimming. I can breathe like a freaking mermaid, Dad."

He didn't say anything, and I could feel his heart racing. He was thinking deeply, but I didn't know what about. It was as if he was trying to find the words. I wanted to get into his head. I wished I could know his thoughts.

"I knew you could breathe under water, yes. I didn't know that *you* knew that you could breathe under water. That's how you survived the accident." His answer shocked me. He knew before I did. He knew and thought I didn't.

"Why didn't you tell me? Why did I have to figure it out on my own?" I didn't give him time to answer, then I got to the real question I wanted to know, "Why did you keep me from Grandma? If you knew about magic and powers and that Grandma wasn't a whack job, why did you keep me from her? She just wanted to protect me from dark magic."

"Your grandma is an amazing woman. I've loved her all my life. But she has secrets, and I was terribly angry when I found out what one of them was. It wasn't until later in my life when I was a dad and had to protect my own kids that I realized she did the best she could for hers."

"What's the secret, Dad?" I asked, suddenly desperate to know and worried that it would change my opinions of her.

"She's a good woman and that is not something for me to tell. I probably shouldn't have even told you there was a secret."

I begged my dad to tell me the secret and he finally told me what it was. He also explained to me the reason he believed Grandma lied about it. I could tell he still respected and loved her. I chose to do the same, even though I didn't think I could handle any more secrets after that. Grandma was a truly kind, loving and intuitive person. But she was also flawed and dang she could keep a secret. If I ever needed to tell her something and didn't want anyone else to know, she would be the person to tell. She was trustworthy in her own way.

At that moment, grandma came in the front door loudly, gasping for air and dropping her things on the floor. The noise startled me and my dad, and we both rose to our feet with questioning looks on our faces.

"We need to find Liv; Ruth says she is missing."

Chapter 56
GRACE

Emily and Bess were waiting at the walking trail near the woods when I walked up with my wagon of junk. Emily had two heavy duty bags of stuff and Bess was carrying a cardboard box under one arm and against her hip. When I reached them, we all stepped off the paved trail and pushed our way through the branches that had grown over since the last time we had been out there. I was excited because we were going to grow as a coven, strengthen our powers and set some junk on fire.

Chapter 57
LIV

Hitchhiking wasn't beneath me, but I decided against it. There was a creepy dude when I left the bus station trying to offer me a ride. I couldn't get a ticket out of town because it was late, and the next bus wouldn't go out until the next morning. Plus, it was only going to another smallish town about twenty miles down the road and that would be no help at all. I wanted to go to Las Vegas, but that bus only left town once a week on Mondays.

First, I considered hitch hiking to a bigger city, like Boston. I was sure a bigger city would probably have buses going to Las Vegas daily, maybe even several a day. I walked away from the bus station with the intent of hitchhiking. That's when I bumped into Mr. Creepy Creeperton.

Mr. Creepy was a little too eager to give me a ride. He said he knew a place we could get dinner on the way. It wasn't his dirty clothes that made me cringe, or the molester glasses he wore. I wasn't even turned off by the tattoos. But he kept doing this clicking thing with his tongue and I overall had a bad feeling about him. I told him politely that I didn't need a ride and that my grandma would bring me back next Monday. I also added that we would be traveling together. I realized after the fact that he probably didn't believe my story anyway. Thankfully, he drove off after telling me it was my loss.

No, it wasn't my loss. I wasn't about to get molested or murdered by some dude at a bus station. Instead, I followed the walking trail down to the woods and camped out in the abandoned shack until Monday. On Monday, I would go back to get my bus ticket to Vegas and hope that Mr. Creepy Creeperton didn't show up expecting me and find me without my grandma. I shivered at the thought.

It was already getting dark as I reached the part of the paved walking trail that met up with the trees. There was an opening between some bushes and trees that we normally used to enter the woods, but everything was grown over since it had been a while. I didn't want to take a chance of Grace or anyone else coming down and finding evidence that I had been there, so I walked further down for about a half an hour and found a gap between some trees. I used my phone's flashlight to see, hoping I wouldn't get lost. I could have gone back to the overgrown bushes so I would be somewhere familiar, but I would meet up with the dirt path eventually.

After an hour of walking and almost calling someone for help, I found the dirt path. By that point, I had been so turned around that I didn't know which way to follow the path. I went right and worst-case scenario would be that I would make it to the other end of the woods and then I could just turn around and walk back the other way until I found the giant rock with the spray-painted peace sign that signaled time to leave the path.

I chose right the first time and quickly found the peace rock. Instinctively, I left the path after the rock until I found the tree with the heart shaped roots, continued for ten minutes and the abandoned cabin was in sight.

Spending the night in the abandoned shack probably wasn't one of my best decisions. It was freezing, even with the small fire I set in the stone fireplace for heat. I was also very sore. My phone was getting low on battery, so I plugged it into my external battery charger. I had finally stopped getting messages from everyone every five seconds, but I did get one here and there every so often. I even got a long heartfelt message from Grace, but I ignored it. I had used up all the firewood the night before, so I collected fallen branches and any wood I could find near the cabin.

The sun was shining bright through the trees, and it was unseasonably warm for November. After I brought the first load of wood back to the cabin, I was sweating in my winter coat and beanie. I took everything off and shoved it in my duffel bag.

Suddenly, branches creaked as they broke in the distance. I held my duffel bag tight to my chest and peeked around the side of the cabin. I was still outside, and the door was on the other end. I did the math in my head trying to determine if I would be able to make it to the door, get myself inside and push something in front of it before whatever animal was out there would catch and devour me.

Determining the odds were not good, I hid instead, hoping the animal wouldn't be able to sniff me out. I ducked behind a bush next to a downed tree and watched toward the noise. More branches broke and footsteps, lots of them, pattered as they came closer. There was also a noise I couldn't make out. It sounded almost like a... wagon? I continued to watch for the source of the sound. After a few seconds, Grace, Emily, and Bess emerged from the trees on the other side of the cabin.

They were pulling a wagon full of wood and metal, Emily had two bags and Bess had a box. They were most likely going to try to burn and melt them using Emily's fire power. Emily had been working on her powers. I even helped her a few times. She was getting stronger. They were probably going to burn the woods down if they weren't careful. I watched them unpack everything near the fire ring.

My phone rang and I quickly pressed the decline button as I fumbled with it, hoping I was able to silence it fast enough.

"Hello? Liv?" A voice came from my phone. Dammit. I accidentally answered it. "Liv, it's Meranda. I just want to know you are safe. Where are you? Everyone is worried?"

"I'm fine," I spoke quietly. "I'm not telling anyone where I am, but you should probably get to the abandoned shack. Your friends are idiots."

Chapter 58
MERANDA

Liv hung up on me and I immediately tried to call Grace. No answer. I tried Bess. No answer. Finally, I tried Emily. She didn't answer either. When I had called Liv, I was already heading to the abandoned cabin. When my grandma came in and told me that Ruth said Liv was missing, I had a feeling she might be at the abandoned cabin. Maybe it was my connection to her as a sister, but I just *felt* she was there.

I told my dad and grandma that I was going to go search a few places for Liv, not telling them where I was going. I didn't even have time to deal with the new information Dad had told me, or to stay behind for when he told her that I knew. I was so focused on finding Liv that I couldn't even think about the secret that was going to blow up my friend's whole life and everything she knew. But I was going to tell her. She had the right to know.

When I called Liv and she said I should probably get to the abandoned shack, I just knew she was there, and I knew what my friends were probably doing. I was surprised that Bess would be a part of it. We had joked about Emily burning the shack and/or the woods down at some point if she practiced her powers there.

We understood it was secluded and no one else seemed to know about the place but it was literally surrounded by stuff that burns. I ran as fast as I could, hoping I would remember the way. I had only been there once with Bess. I kept saying it in my head. *Dirt path, peace rock, heart roots, five minutes past, smashed metal barrel with a tree through it, open to a clearing and find the old well.*

There was a nagging feeling that something terrible was about to happen and I was filled with adrenaline. I ran so hard that my chest burned terribly. My windpipe dried from the inside out as I breathed. I found the slightly disturbed overgrown branches and went in, following the dirt path. *Peace Rock. Peace Rock. Peace Rock.*

Realizing I couldn't stop or slow down, I ran harder. A branch whipped me in the face, and I cried out, reaching up to touch it, tears instantly streaming down my face. It stung even with all the adrenaline coursing through me. It stung and burned. I was reminded of why I was running and found my second wind. There it was. The Peace Rock. *Heart roots. Heart roots. Heart roots.*

I continued running, searching for the roots shaped like a heart. I found them and was very hopeful I'd make it in time. I was almost there. Afraid of what I would find, I made it to the smashed barrel and found my way to the clearing. I could see it. Not the old well, but the smoke. I smelled it, then the flames appeared in my view.

Chapter 59
GRACE

When we arrived at the shack, we made two piles. One for items to burn such as wood and one to melt such as metal. Between the three of us, we had two decent size piles. The burn pile was bigger than the melt pile, though. We used the well to get a bucket of water. It was brown and nasty looking, but we weren't going to drink it. It was only a safety precaution. Really, Emily should have been able to put out any fire she started with her magic.

"Okay, Emily. Show us what you can do," I said, waving my hand toward the two piles. Emily inspected the piles and chose a few items from each, carrying her handful over to the fire ring and setting them down next to it.

"Let's start with conjuring fire," she said, placing the wooden items that consisted of a broken broom handle, a scrap piece of 2x4 and the back of a small chair, next to the fire ring.

"Do you need us to do anything?" Bess asked, stepping toward Emily.

"Nah, I got this. Just watch, I need to focus," Emily said, pinching the fingers of her right hand together. She held up her hand, closed her eyes for a few seconds, then opened them. A small flame danced over the tips of her fingers.

"That's great!" I said, quietly but excitedly clapping my hands. My chest warmed with pride.

"This is where I have trouble, as soon as I move my hand the fire usually goes out."

Emily moved her fingers trying to cup the fire in the palm of her hand and it went out.

"That's okay. Try it again," Bess said. I felt a twinge of disappointment in my chest.

Emily pinched her fingers, closed her eyes, and took a deep breath. When she opened them, a flame bounced at the tips of her fingers. I felt the warmth in my chest again. It was okay. She just needed practice. When she moved her fingers, the flame went out again.

With our encouragement, Emily tried again several times. On the seventh time, she moved her fingers and the flame stayed. As she cupped it in her hand, the flame formed a ball shape.

"Can you throw it?" I asked, excitedly.

"Well, maybe, but where? I don't want to start anything on fire."

"Okay, how about..." I looked around at the shack and the surrounding trees, "hmmm... oh, how about this?" I picked up the chair back, the scrap 2x4 and the broken broom handle and placed it in the fire ring.

Emily wound up like she was about to pitch a soft ball and threw the fireball into the ring. There was a cracking noise that startled the three of us, then the fire spread over the three wooden items in the ring.

"They're burning!" I cheered!

"Wow! Em, that is awesome! Can you put it out now?" Bess asked.

"Maybe," Emily laughed. "It usually goes out on its own. But I will try, let me focus."

Emily stood next to the fire ring, took a deep breath, and closed her eyes. She opened her eyes and focused on the flames. Bess and I watched the fire as it slowly extinguished. A single line of smoke was all that remained. The three of us jumped up and down screaming excitedly and Bess gave Emily a high five.

"We should try something bigger," I said.

"We have a whole pile of stuff to try," Bess said.

"I was thinking bigger than that, even," I said, staring at the shack.

"You're crazy. No way am I burning a building down!" Emily said and Bess shook her head at me.

"Guys, this shack is abandoned. We are the only ones who ever come here. Probably the only ones who even know it's here. Nobody will miss it. Nobody will care. And besides, Emily will put the fire out right away. There probably wouldn't even be much damage," I said trying to convince them. If Emily could pull it off, we had an even bigger chance of successfully summoning my grandmother.

"This is the first fire bigger than a candle flame that I have been able to put out. What if I can't do it?" Emily asked, concern showing on her face.

"You can do it," I turned to Bess. "Right? She can do it can't she?" Then I turned back to Emily. "We are both here to support you. You can do it. This is huge and you are amazing!"

"She's right. You can do it and we are both here. You aren't going to burn the woods down. We will put it out right away," Bess said.

"Fine. I will try it," Emily said, standing to face the shack.

Bess and I stood on either side of her. Emily took a deep breath and closed her eyes. Then she opened them and focused on her fingers pinched upward in front of her. A small flame flickered at the tips of her fingers. We all took a deep breath together as Emily focused on the flame, slowly moving her fingers to cup the flame in her palm. The flame formed into a ball on the first try, as she held it in her hand.

"Here goes nothing," Emily said, as she wound up the pitch. "One... two... THREE!!"

Emily threw the fireball toward the roof of the shack. It cracked loudly on impact and started to burn. Just then, three crows came out of nowhere and dove down at us. We moved out of the way and instinctively covered our heads with our arms. Emily screamed.

"My spirit animal. There's something wrong. They are warning us. Hurry put the fire out!" Bess yelled.

The wood on the shack turned white in some places as the fire pulled every ounce of moisture out of it. On the ground next to the shack was a Holy Orchard High Swim beanie. I immediately recognized the logo surrounded in blue. The hat Liv wore all the time lately.

"Oh, my Goddess! Liv is in there!" Emily cried, noticing it at the same time as I did.

"PUT THE FIRE OUT!" Bess yelled, as she and I both ran toward the shack and tried to peer in the windows.

"I can't see anything! I have to go in!" I yelled, running for the door. I was terrified and I felt extremely guilty. What if I killed my best friend in a fire? This was *my* dumb ass idea.

"PUT THE FIRE OUT!!" Bess screamed more frantically, as she threw the bucket of water at the roof. The flames were spreading over the shack and there was no time to lose. The door to the shack came into the kitchen. Smoke was coming from the ceiling, and I lowered myself to the floor. Emily and Bess yelled frantically as I searched for Liv, calling out her name. Bess came in behind me just as the roof collapsed over our only exit.

Chapter 60
MERANDA

When the shack came into sight, it was on fire. Emily stood outside and Bess was about to go in. I yelled for her to not go inside but she didn't hear. I couldn't see Grace anywhere. I ran as fast as I could and felt like I might pass out. The roof over the door collapsed and everyone was screaming. Liv was suddenly there holding onto Emily by her shoulders and saying something to her. I was finally close enough to hear.

"You can do this. Put the fire out. I will help you. I will summon water. Keep trying!" Liv yelled, her voice shaking. She glanced up and saw me. "Summon water with me! Hurry!"

Liv and I held onto Emily and chanted, "Put the fire out. Put the fire out." I stared at the flames engulfing the shack and pictured water droplets pulling together from the air, sucking out of what was left of grass and leaves. I directed it toward the flames on the shack. "Put the fire out. Put the fire out."

There was a hissing sound and all at once the fire stopped with only a little bit of smoke left behind. The door was blocked, but the three of us pulled the weak and broken wood apart from one side of the shack until there was an opening big enough for one of us to fit inside. We all peeked in thinking the worst, but Grace and Bess were on the other side of the wall making their way to the opening.

"Are you okay?" I yelled.

"Yes, completely fine. No damage at all," Bess said.

"How?" I asked, tears forming behind my eyes, but ever so grateful that they were okay.

"Bess used her power and summoned a bubble of air to keep the fire away from us so that we could breathe. It was amazing. I am so sorry," Grace sobbed and reached her arms out to hug Liv.

"I'm so glad you came," Liv said to me, putting her arms around Grace and hugging her tightly.

"I was already on my way searching for you," I said to Liv.

"Why? Why would you come looking for me after knowing that I was the reason for your mom's death and I killed our brother because I'm an idiot," Liv sobbed.

"You aren't responsible for the accident. It's a curse on all Wickstrom witches. We are destined to be alone. I was afraid the curse had come for me when I got here and Bess was in the shack," I hugged Bess tightly and kissed her forehead. I would have to break up with her, but I'd worry about that later.

Liv pulled back from hugging Grace. "Why is summoning your grandma so important? You risked everyone's lives today. It's not only your fault, but *dang* what is this all for?"

The fire was out, and everyone was safe, at least for that moment. Grace motioned for us to all sit down and we huddled close together in a circle, like we always did.

"When my grandma was still alive, she told me there was a secret that even my mom didn't know. She said when she believed I was old enough and strong enough in my power she was going to tell me. Part of my strength was being able to wait, but after she died, I lost my patience. If even my mom didn't know, how would I ever find out what the secret was? I did research and found out that some witches can summon the dead," Grace put her head down and looked ashamed. Liv put her arm around Grace and hugged her tight.

"If it helps at all, I forgive you for everything. Keeping secrets only makes things harder for us. Meranda deserved to know I was her sister," Liv said, staring up at me as if to say she was sorry to me, too, but she didn't say the words.

"You know, I tried summoning my grandma myself so many times. Every time I was closer to doing it. I just wanted to ask her one question, *what's the secret?* I don't even know if it's something big or something I need to discover for myself like I am amazing and powerful on my own. This could have been for nothing, but I just wanted to see her and talk to her," Grace said.

"You are powerful and amazing on your own. You don't give yourself enough credit for it. You were so focused on everyone else getting stronger in their powers so we could be strong as a coven, but what about your own powers? You should have been focusing on yourself," Liv said.

I was saddened because everyone in my family was destined to lose their love. I was pained over the idea of breaking Bess's heart, but even more over the thought of losing her in some horrible way if we stayed together. Liv's speech about secrets making things harder for everyone really struck a chord in me. I needed to tell them what my dad told me.

"Speaking of secrets..." everyone looked up at me waiting for what I had to say. "I found out another big one today. It's pretty huge."

"Okay, enough with the suspense, just say it," Liv demanded.

"I found out the real reason my dad left Holy Orchard and kept me from my grandma. He found out a secret and it involves one of you."

Liv glared at me as if to tell me to get on with it.

"So, I think all of you know that my grandma had a baby named Sarah who died in infancy. That is where I got my middle name," I said as a question. Everyone nodded, so I continued. "It turns out that Sarah didn't really die."

"Woah!" Bess shouted.

"Holy crap!" Grace yelled.

"How is your life a soap opera?" Emily asked.

"So where is she?" Liv asked.

"Well, alive and well in Holy Orchard. And we all know her and have spent time with her," I said, stopping to breathe because I was lightheaded. "One of us knows her extremely well."

"Who??!" everyone asked simultaneously, leaning closer to me.

I had to be sensitive with this info and part of me was having second thoughts about telling the group. Maybe I should have pulled her aside and told her privately. Everyone was giving me an impatient stare.

"Well?!" Bess asked.

"Grace's mom."

Chaos erupted as everyone started freaking out and talking at once. Grace looked at me confused like she didn't understand what I said. Her eyes were asking me to repeat myself and explain.

"Woah, okay. Let me explain it all. So, my dad overheard a conversation with my grandma and Grace's grandma Sophie. They were talking about the babies they had switched. Grandma's baby didn't die. Sophie's did."

"No way!" Bess said.

"I believe it. With all the secrets we've found out already, I'm not surprised," Liv said.

Grace was silent, stunned even. She seemed deep in thought like she was trying to piece it together.

"My grandma and Sophie had their daughters only days apart. But Sophie's baby died. She had no other children and had a hard labor and delivery. The doctor told her she wouldn't be able to have any more babies. They were best friends and in the same coven. My grandma's family had a curse on them. She was devastated by the loss of her husband Samuel and hoped that if she gave Sarah to Sophie that not only would Sophie get to raise a child and not break her husband's heart, but that she would also maybe possibly be able to escape the curse on the Wickstrom family. You know, if she wasn't raised a Wickstrom. They never told anyone. They were the only ones who knew. Even Sophie's husband never knew."

Grace looked like she was incredibly surprised but also like she finally understood. The realization was all over her face.

"I bet that was the secret Grandma was going to tell me. And being raised as someone else didn't stop the curse. My dad died in a plane crash. My mom is destined to be alone, and I guess that means I am, too.

Chapter 61
GRACE

My mother loved my father, and they were together for fifteen years. Maybe they didn't get to be together forever, but they got to be together for a while. They had a great love, and they were happy. I didn't want my mother to ever stop trying to find that again, so it was best not to tell her that she was Sarah Wickstrom. She loved my grandmother, and I didn't want to destroy her memory.

I always had a close relationship with Mrs. Wickstrom because she and my grandmother Sophie were best friends and we lived next door. All this time she knew I was her granddaughter. I had always felt closer to her and although I was lied to, I wasn't mad. She tried to protect my mother and give her a better life with love and happiness.

After the fire that could almost have killed me and my friends, I needed to stop trying to do things for myself and on my own. The coven really needed to work together as a group and make decisions together. We were already stronger, knowing the connections we had. Liv and Meranda were sisters. I was their cousin, so that meant we had a coven with THREE Wickstrom witches. Bess and Emily were two amazing friends with kick-ass powers. We were positive that we would find a way, somehow to break this curse. If not for our generation, for the next.

Chapter 62
MERANDA

Grandma knew her secret would get out eventually. She admitted that she knew Liv was Dad's daughter but only found out after suspecting it and confronting Liv's mom. By time she found out, Dad was living in Hawaii and married with one child and another on the way. He was also not speaking to her at the time and too much time had passed for it to be a good idea to tell him. Dad had forgiven her and so had I. She had the best of intentions and she assured us that as far as she knew, there were no more secrets in the Wickstrom family.

Grace didn't want to tell her mom that she was Sarah Wickstrom and Grandma agreed. So much time had passed, and Grandma only wanted the best for her daughter. Grace's mom already had a close relationship with Grandma without knowing she was her mom. We all agreed, it was for the best not to ruin anything.

As for Bess, the first time we got together after the fire, I found the nerve to break up with her, or so I believed. We had decided to meet up at the shack. Somehow, that half-burnt abandoned shack used to be inhabited by someone. We joked about the people who may have lived there. It was a couple and they left because they had a child and needed to live closer to town. The shack was where they lived and fell deeper in love and conceived their child. We called it the *love shack*. It was super cheesy, but we laughed every time we thought about it.

I was there first, because we decided it would be better to meet there rather than walk up together. She looked terrified because she knew what the meeting was for. She knew I was going to end things. But she was beautiful as always. I would lose my nerve in the time it would take to walk there together, so I was glad I arrived first.

We could cry and console each other on the walk back, but it had to be done. I couldn't stay with her and seal her fate. Wickstrom witches were cursed and destined to be alone, losing their loves to death. The idea of losing Bess in some awful way tortured me ever since the day I read about the curse. I imagined her getting hit by a car or coming down with some terrible illness, drowning like my mom and Rocco or dying in a fire. I truly believed I was losing her the day of the shack fire. I should have ended things right then rather than be selfish enough to risk her life another minute, but I couldn't. I couldn't break her heart, moments after she almost died.

It took several minutes for her to reach me, from the moment she emerged onto the clearing. The wait was torture. The anticipation killed me. I didn't want to, but I had to. I knew it and I knew she knew it, too. It was awkward for both of us when she finally reached me. It felt like we were already broken up. We both said "hi" then stood in silence for several moments, each of us waiting for the other person to speak first. Finally, I broke the silence.

"So, I guess we both know why we are here," I said, my voice cracked on "here."

"What if I cry and beg you not to?" she asked, biting her cherry glossed lips.

"You know why we have to..." I couldn't say the words in that moment. I couldn't say "break up."

"I don't care. I don't want to stop being us," she said, eyes glossy as she reached for me.

"No," I said, my eyes teared up as I lost the ability to speak.

"Your parents were together almost twenty years. Grace's parents were together for fifteen years. It's worth the risk. Even if I die in a month, at least I would have been happy with you. I could die any time for any reason, and it might not even have anything to do with any Wickstrom curse. I should be able to decide what I do while I am alive. I don't care, I just want to be happy. I just want to be with you," she said it all in one breath then she gasped and cried loudly.

It broke my heart when she cried. I hated it. I fell so hard for her over a matter of months and I loved her, more than I ever loved anyone. More than Leilani, my first love that took years to build. I could feel it in my bones and every part of me. I loved Bess and she was my person. She was right and wrong at the same time. She *should* be able to choose, but I didn't want her to die. I didn't want to lose her. How would I convince her to be okay with breaking up?

"I love you," I said, hugging her and kissing her forehead. She was a few inches shorter than me, and she hugged her face into my neck. "We have to break up."

"No!" she cried. "This isn't fair!"

I pulled away from her and held her at arms' length from me. I gazed into her eyes.

"Please, don't break my heart?" She cried.

"I have to. I would always worry that something was going to happen to you. Anytime you don't answer my text? Any time you leave, or I don't know where you are, I will think something has happened to you. We wouldn't be happy like that. Right?" She didn't answer me, so I repeated myself, "Right?!"

"No, it doesn't have to be like that. You can learn to forget about it. Maybe we can find a spell to forget that we know about the curse," she bargained.

"No, that is ridiculous, and you know it," I said, getting frustrated.

"We can get comfortable again. You won't always worry. It will be fine."

"No!"

She grabbed my face and kissed me hard at first, but then both of our lips softened at the contact of one another. I didn't want to stop. I couldn't stop. We kissed long and passionately, like we were savoring it. Like we would never get to experience another kiss like that again. Leaves and brush and wood pieces swirled around us. I could smell the sweet earth and feel the air as Bess and I continued to kiss. I breathed it in as I hugged her tight to me. It took all of my strength to pull away from the kiss and stop. She just stared into my eyes like she was begging me to change my mind. It could always be like this if we were together, but we would always have that curse hovering above us like a dark cloud. I hugged her tight and looked down. We were floating and had been floating the whole time.

I was breaking up with the girl who made me float. The girl who swirled apples and leaves around us when we kissed. There was so much more we could do and be together. I broke down and cried out loud. I thought I would never stop when I heard her voice ever so softly.

"What if we figure out how to break the curse?"

About the Author

Amy lives in Northern Minnesota with her wife Sandy, her cats (Cowboy, Prince Henry, Batman, and Carlos), and her dog (Ruby.) She has spent over 3 decades being fascinated by witches, both mythical and real. She has traveled to Salem, Massachusetts, and other cities on the East Coast to learn more about the history of witches. During her research, Amy has only become more immersed in the culture and history of witches and witchcraft. You can expect to read about witches and other magical beings in her future writing projects. Amy is an honors graduate of Southern New Hampshire University where she earned a Bachelor's Degree in Psychology with a concentration in Forensic Psychology, a Master's in English and Creative Writing, and an MFA in Creative Writing. She has had 3 poems and a short story published in *The Penmen Review*.

Read more at amysouthard.com.